107043

Kirk, Michael,
pseud

10.00

Dragonship

DRAGONSHIP

As Michael Kirk

DRAGONSHIP
ALL OTHER PERILS

As Bill Knox

RALLY TO KILL
WHITEWATER
DRAW BATONS!
STORMTIDE
SEAFIRE
TO KILL A WITCH
WHO SHOT THE BULL
BLUEBACK
THE TALLEYMAN
FIGUREHEAD
JUSTICE ON THE ROCKS
BLACKLIGHT
THE GHOST CAR
DEVILWEED
THE TASTE OF PROOF
THE SCAVENGERS
THE KILLING GAME
THE DRUM OF UNGARA
THE GREY SENTINELS
LITTLE DROPS OF BLOOD
IN AT THE KILL
LEAVE IT TO THE HANGMAN

As Noah Webster

A WITCHDANCE IN BAVARIA
A BURIAL IN PORTUGAL
A KILLING IN MALTA
FLICKERING DEATH

DRAGONSHIP

MICHAEL KIRK

PUBLISHED FOR THE CRIME CLUB BY
DOUBLEDAY & COMPANY, INC.
GARDEN CITY, NEW YORK
1977

All of the characters in this book are fictitious, and any resemblance to actual persons, living or dead, is purely coincidental.

Library of Congress Cataloging in Publication Data

Knox, Bill, 1928–
Dragonship.

I. Title.
PZ4.K748Dn3   [PR6061.N6]   823'.9'14

ISBN: 0-385-12152-0
Library of Congress Catalog Card Number: 76-18355
Copyright © 1976 by Bill Knox
Printed in the United States of America
First Edition in the United States of America

For Allan and Margaret

'In the name of God, Amen.

Be it known that, with regard to the schedule attaching to and forming part of this policy, the Assured as well in their own Name, as for and in the Name and Names of all and every other Person or Persons to whom the same doth, may or shall appertain, in part or in all, doth make Assurance and cause themselves and them and every of them, to be assured, lost or not lost, at and from the Ports or Places named in the Voyage upon any kind of Goods and Merchandises, in the good Ship or Vessel as named, whosoever is Master, under God, for this present voyage, beginning the Adventure upon the said Goods and Merchandises from the loading thereon aboard the said ship . . .'

Extract from standard, current international marine-cargo insurance policy.

DRAGONSHIP

CHAPTER ONE

The breeze was warm, from the south end of the summer Baltic. It ruffled the sea, kissed the Copenhagen shoreline, and filled the brightly coloured nylon spinnakers of a flotilla of small sailboats which were close in on the Danish side of the Øresund Strait. They were turning on a marker for the homeward leg of an afternoon's racing, with the Swedish coastline a low blur on the eastern horizon behind them.

Andrew Laird watched their sleek shapes from the cockpit of the blunt-bowed harbour launch which was taking him out to a job he didn't relish. The leading sailboat foamed past the launch's stern, cutting through the slack propellor wash, a vast orange spinnaker snatching all the wind it could. A girl in a bikini was at the helm, another girl and a couple of men were laughing as they crouched low on the heeling deck, and he could have bet the return half of his air ticket that they had a case of beer cooling somewhere aboard.

"*Ja*, they have a good time." The shirt-sleeved, middle-aged boatman spat appreciatively over the side, allowing for the wind, then grunted and nodded ahead. "But the rest of us have to work, eh?"

"*Tak* . . . thanks," said Laird bleakly, his small daydream dissolving. "I hadn't forgotten, believe me."

The boatman chuckled, spun the wheel, and sent the launch curving in towards the ship that lay at anchor ahead.

Her name was the *Velella*, ten thousand tons of modern general-cargo carrier, and thirty-six hours before she had sailed from Copenhagen for Boston via London under the command of Captain James Sloan, a rough-tongued, totally efficient Australian. Panamanian registered for tax purposes, she was owned by the Raymond Line, a Greek syndicate.

And now she was back, light blue hull blackened and scorched from fo'c'sle to midships, her captain dead, several of her crew injured. A yellow and blue Keep Clear warning flag flapped sadly above the blistered paint of her mainmast and a tug and fireboat lay alongside like anxious nurses.

A sudden fire had raged like an inferno aboard the *Velella*, beginning deep in number-one hold. It had spread to number-two hold, and only been quelled by the final, desperate decision to flood both. The clanking pumps at work on the tug and fireboat were now helping to suck out the tons of water which had deluged in when that had happened.

Laird grimaced to himself at other details as the launch steered towards a companionway ladder near the cargo ship's stern. Several hull plates had buckled under the intense heat. Porthole glasses were cracked and shattered, a lifeboat hung like a blackened skeleton from one pair of grotesquely twisted davits, and the radio aerial was a temporary jury-rig affair.

"They had it bad, eh?" said the boatman conversationally. *"Nej,* not for me. I been a ferry-boat sailor twenty years an' home every night. Better that way, I think." He frowned up at the ship, then cut the launch's speed until they were barely drifting in. "Do I wait for you?"

"Yes. I won't be too long." Laird left it at that.

"Okay." The boatman refused to be curious about his passenger's business. He had enough worries of his own, starting with a wife who had decided she would stop sharing his bed till she got more housekeeping money. "I charge by the half hour."

Laird smiled a little and nodded. One more minor item on his expense sheet wasn't going to make much difference in a day which had brought him by jet from London to Copenhagen, then out to the smouldering ship.

The *Velella* had become a major insurance claim. As a marine claims adjuster with Clanmore Alliance, a London-based insurance firm as canny as its name, Laird had plenty of work ahead.

The launch reached the dangling ladder, bumped briefly against the hull, and Laird grabbed for a side rope. He got a foot on the nearest rung, swung himself up, and began climbing as the little launch eased clear again.

"What do you want, mister?" came a shout as he topped the ladder. One hand still on the side rope, Laird saw one of the *Velella*'s junior officers hurrying along the deck towards him. His uniform was stained and singed, his young face was tired and smoke-blackened, and as he reached Laird he backed the question with a scowled warning. "If you're a newsman, get back down or we'll heave you over."

"I'm on ship's business," said Laird soothingly, conscious of a large, equally grimy seaman making an unfriendly approach from the other side. He pulled his identification pass from an inside pocket and showed it. "Your owners said they'd let you know I was coming."

"Clanmore—yes, they did." The tired young face relaxed a little. "Sorry, Mr. Laird. I'm Dave Hunter, the third mate. That wasn't much of a welcome but we've been fighting off an assortment of vultures since we got in."

"I can guess," said Laird softly. "Who's in command?"

"Our chief officer—Sean Peters." Hunter shook his head with a dazed respect. "He's the only reason we got back."

"And Captain Sloan?" probed Laird. "Just what did happen when he was killed?"

"The word came back that the fire was getting out of control in number-one hold, and he went down to help," said Hunter wearily. "The chief officer was already there with our full firefighting team, but Captain Sloan tried to get one of the hoselines in closer, on his own—" He stopped and shrugged. "A whole damned stack of burning cargo collapsed on top of him."

"That's the part I didn't know," said Laird grimly. "I left before the full reports were in."

"He must have been killed instantly," said Hunter, making it a hope, and drew a deep breath. "Sean Peters dived in and dragged him out—got burned himself doing it— but the Old Man was dead by then." He shrugged again. "I'll go and find Chief Officer Peters. He's below somewhere. Better stay right here, Mr. Laird—it isn't safe to stray around."

The young third mate went away, going down a companionway stair to a lower deck. Laird stayed where he was, gave a sympathetic nod to the large seaman who was still hovering, and took a long, slow look around.

From midships aft the *Velella* appeared undamaged. But chaos began just for'ard of the bridge superstructure, where the steel deck was covered with a litter of snaking hosepipes, sodden strips of canvas, and charred fragments of broken wood.

Both for'ard holds had their hatch covers open, the hoselines disappearing into their dark, gaping maws while the pumps clanked on. Some Danish firemen were working around the hatches, obviously helping other men already down below.

Suddenly, as he watched, a fireman in a smoke helmet appeared at the lip of number-one hold and gestured frantically. Behind him, a thin haze of smoke began building.

There were shouts, the clanking pumps stopped, and a group of firemen hurried forward with a hose jet. They went into action on the lip of the hold and the smoke gave way to a hissing cloud of steam. Then it was over. More firemen were going down into the hold, and the pumps resumed their steady beat.

Laird whistled softly. The *Velella*'s problems weren't over. After any fire at sea there was always the chance of more than one smouldering remnant of damaged cargo being ready to burst into flames again, no matter how safe things might appear.

Still waiting, he felt the summer wind ruffling his hair and considered the sparkling blue water thoughtfully. At least the weather had favoured ship and crew. To have to cope with storm conditions as well as fire would have been an even greater nightmare.

He heard footsteps and turned. The man coming towards him was small in stature, but broad-built, with short, spiky red hair, a coarse stubble of beard framing a plump face which at that moment held no particular welcome. Left hand heavily bandaged, wearing a crumpled white open-necked shirt with grimy khaki slacks and what looked like a pair of old baseball boots, he stopped a few paces short of Laird, looked him up and down, then gave a nod.

"Don't expect me to say welcome aboard, Laird," said the man bleakly in a nasal, Liverpool accent. "I had a signal about you all right—but it didn't particularly brighten my day."

"Chief Officer Peters?" asked Laird carefully, the reception being more or less what he'd expected.

"Right." The *Velella*'s first mate took another step nearer. "Look, man, it's nothing personal. But I've too many real problems on my plate to give a damn about insurance paperwork." The plump, unshaven face shaped a scowl. "What the hell's all the rush anyway? Are your bosses so keen to trim down claims they can't wait?"

Laird grinned. "They don't exactly throw their money around, but you've got the rest of it wrong. Your owners pay their premiums, so someone like me turns up." He held out his hand. "I'm this week's free offer from Clanmore, no strings attached, Chief Officer. I've no magic wand, but I'm here to help—and the paperwork can wait."

The other man hesitated, then his round face thawed a little and he took Laird's hand with a grip like that of a powerful bearpaw.

"That's different," he admitted. "The way things are, I'd take help from the Earl of Hell himself. You said no strings?"

"None."

"Settled." Peters switched his gaze for'ard. "She's sound enough below the waterline and we've almost finished pumping out—in fact, we're checking our way through both holds now. If the Danes give us harbour clearance we'll have her docked in Copenhagen by tonight."

"When that happens, you've a crew who look like they could sleep the clock round," said Laird. He considered Peters again, then added, "I'd say that goes for you too."

"Maybe." Peters grimaced, as if sleep were a luxury he'd forgotten about. "If I get the chance—the Danes may have other ideas."

"Why?" Laird raised a surprised eyebrow.

"We've a passenger missing," said Peters wearily. "Gone, vanished—God knows how. They don't like it."

"I didn't know," said Laird slowly.

"We weren't sure for a spell ourselves." The other man gave a long sigh. "We had Captain Sloan dead, two deck-hands with multiple burns—they're in hospital ashore now—and a ship to try to save. In the middle of it all, a passenger just disappears—jumps over the side for all I know. That's not going to look good on the records, is it?"

"The word is you did a good job, saved this ship, Chief," said Laird deliberately. "And I heard how you hurt that arm."

"Then we've a third mate who talks too much," grunted Peters. He fell silent, his tired eyes scrutinising Laird again.

Andrew Laird was the kind of man most people decided to judge carefully. Nudging thirty years of age and over medium height, he had a stocky muscular build which partly disguised the fact. His hair was dark and thick, prematurely streaked with grey around the temples, and he had the kind of face which at first appeared hard-set, until he smiled, when it could become boyish. Grey-green eyes went with a nose which had been broken and reset at some time, he had a mouth which puckered easily, and his voice held a Scottish wisp.

He wore a lightweight grey suit with a faded blue shirt and a knitted dark blue tie. His feet were in brown casual shoes and his open jacket gave a glimpse of a plaited leather belt with a seaman's heavy brass buckle.

Sean Peters took it all in, noted hands that were strong and long-fingered, and sensed something else.

"You've had some seatime of your own, right?"

"Some," admitted Laird. "Radio mainly, not deck."

"Better than nothing." Peters made up his mind. "I've

a bottle in my cabin. I talk better over a drink—and I need one."

Laird followed him along the deck, then up a ladder, through a companionway, and into the living quarters below the bridge area. They passed the captain's cabin, then Peters opened a door on the port side and gestured Laird in.

"My place." Peters followed him in, then heeled the door shut with a sigh of relief. Going over to a locker, he opened it and brought out a bottle and glasses. "Whisky?"

"Fine." Laird glanced around the cabin as Peters spun the cap from the bottle and began pouring.

The chief officer of the *Velella* had comfortable quarters. His bunk was under the cabin porthole, a small desk stood against one bulkhead, he had plenty of locker space, and there was a compact, well-filled bookcase. That left plenty of room to spare for a couple of armchairs on a central square of carpet, while an open door gave a glimpse of a small, private bathroom. But the bunk hadn't been slept in and a uniform jacket which had been discarded beside the bunk had the left sleeve partially burned away.

Laird noticed one thing more as Peters finished pouring the drinks. Pride of place on the desk was given to a framed photograph of an attractive, middle-aged woman and two school-age boys.

"Here." Peters shoved a well-filled glass into Laird's hand, went back for his own glass, and took a long swallow without any preliminaries. Then, waving Laird into one of the chairs, he slumped into the other—an exhausted, moody man who stared at what was left of his drink without really seeing it.

"The Danes took Jimmy Sloan's body ashore," he said heavily. "They say they'll need a routine autopsy—but they'll let me know as soon as we can make arrangements."

"How long had you sailed with him?" asked Laird.

"Three years. We got along all right," said Peters gruffly.

"I've heard worse obituaries," said Laird, understanding something more behind the words. He sipped his own drink. "You'd better tell me what you can about your missing passenger."

"It isn't much." The first mate shifted uneasily at the reminder. "He's on the passenger list as Olaf Hansen, a salesman, with a business address in Copenhagen. According to our cabin steward, he was in his late twenties, and the quiet type. He came aboard just before we sailed—I didn't meet him."

Laird nodded. Passengers on a cargo ship couldn't expect VIP treatment. There was too much work for the crew after the ship left port for them to do much more than notice that there were passengers around.

"We had six passengers this trip," said Peters, as if reading his mind. "Hansen and another character were booked to London only, the other four were going with us to Boston. They seemed the usual mix—people who wanted a sea crossing as a change from routine or maybe because they were scared of the big iron birds." He gave a short, humourless laugh. "Well, they backed a loser this time."

"Let me check it through," mused Laird. "You sailed from Copenhagen at—"

"At sixteen hundred hours on Monday," finished Peters for him.

Laird nodded. "The fire was detected at 0400 on Tuesday, twelve hours later. You got back here just after 0400 this morning, another twenty-four hours."

He stopped, realising that Peters wasn't listening, that his attention had switched. Then, after a moment or two, he understood why. The throbbing background clank of the pumps had ended outside, leaving only the slow, muted creaking of the ship as she rode at her anchor on the gentle swell.

"Finished." Peters glanced at a wall clock on the bulkhead near his bunk. "On time, too—that's more than I hoped." He relaxed a little more. "You wanted to know what happened over Hansen, right?"

"Yes."

Laird waited.

"I had the bridge watch when the detector alarm went for a fire in number-one hold. So"—Peters took a quick gulp from his glass—"I roused the Old Man, turned the watch over to the second mate, and went down with the firefighting party."

"Did you give any order about the passengers?"

"Yes, the usual emergency drill. The steward went to wake them and tell them to dress but stay put. Except most of them were already up and about, trying to find out what was going on. He had to round them up before he discovered Hansen was missing."

"So what did you do about it?" prodded Laird.

"Nothing much." Peters flushed to the roots of his spiky red hair. "Hell, the fire was out of control and had reached number-two hold, the Old Man was dead, we'd two men injured. A stray passenger was incidental. Look, I had a Mayday signal going out on our radio saying we might have to abandon ship—"

"But instead you took a gamble and flooded the for'ard holds," mused Laird. "It worked, you beat the fire." He kept his manner neutral. "Well, it cost any cargo the flames hadn't reached, but I'd say it was worth it—you saved maybe three million pounds worth of ship and probably another half million in cargo in the aft holds." Then he gave

Peters a twinkling glance. "I'd say you're due a gold star for enterprise."

"Stuff your gold star," said Peters thickly.

"You'll maybe even get our chairman's special letter of thanks and a presentation watch—he has a contact who gets them wholesale." Laird grinned a little. "Chief, you don't need me to pat you on the back. Let's stick with passenger Hansen. How soon did you search the ship?"

"As soon as things settled down a little." Peters shifted uncomfortably.

"Then what?"

"A couple of ships had answered our Mayday calls. It —well, it was a calm sea and I thought that if he'd gone overboard he might have a chance." Peters paused and shrugged. "I asked one of the ships to search back along our course. The other ship stayed with us for a spell—but we didn't do any searching on our own, not in the state we were in."

"You keep talking about him going overboard." Laird frowned, and saw the man's puzzled reaction. "Well, isn't there another possibility—that he got caught up in the fire?"

"Not a chance," said Peters positively. "Any passenger straying near it would have been seen—and sent packing."

"In the middle of all that was going on?" Laird showed his disbelief, but sensed he wasn't going to get any further. "Let's leave it for now. You said you could use help. What have you got in mind?"

"A couple of things straight off." Finishing his drink, the *Velella*'s first mate got up and used his empty glass like a pointer. "The Danes say they'll run an investigation of their own into the fire, and a Sergeant Lundgard from their harbour police has the job. He's aboard now. I can't stop him, but I want him off my back."

"And if I do that, you'll have a bonus. I'll be out of

your way too?" Laird showed his amusement at the same time as he again uprated the bulky, determined little man standing over him. "All right, I'll try. What else?"

"An easier business. One of the other passengers we had aboard is Jimmy Sloan's niece." Peters showed a slight embarrassment. "All five of them were taken ashore soon after we anchored. Look, I'd like it if you could go along and see that she's all right. Tell her I'll be along as soon as I can."

"Got an address for her?" queried Laird, feeling he was getting off lightly.

"Yes." Peters propped the empty glass against his bandaged arm and used his free hand to fish a slip of paper from his shirt pocket. "She said she'd be at this hotel—her name is Karen Leslie."

"I'll see her." Laird tucked the scrap of paper away. "Chief, mind if I ask you something?"

"Go ahead." Peters started over towards the whisky bottle with his empty glass.

"Why come back to Copenhagen?" asked Laird bluntly. "If I'd had a badly damaged ship I'd have headed for the nearest port that had a repair yard—and this wasn't the nearest."

"Owners' instructions." Peters laid his glass down beside the bottle and didn't look around. "The Raymond Line have a fat shareholding in a Danish repair yard." His voice thickened. "I queried it. They radioed back that I'd already reported my injured weren't on the critical list—and that they hoped they'd be able to confirm I was being appointed captain."

"Like if you want to be master of the *Velella,* shut up?" Laird wasn't surprised. The Raymond Line hadn't a reputation for humanitarian instincts. "Are you captain?"

"They haven't said yet." Peters left the glass empty and

turned, his eyes straying to the photograph on his desk. "Are you married, Laird?"

"No." Andrew Laird gave a lopsided grin. "I stumbled once, but didn't quite fall."

"I am, with kids." Peters' voice sounded very tired. "That way, you think twice before you tell your boss to go to hell."

The buzz of the cabin telephone stopped the first mate there. He went over, scooped up the receiver, and barked an answer. Then Laird saw the man's expression change to near incredulity as he listened.

"Give me that again," he rasped.

The tinny voice at the other end repeated its noises.

"I'll be down." Peters hung up violently, drew a deep breath, and faced Laird. "You'd better see this. They've found a body in number-one hold."

"Your passenger?" Laird scrambled to his feet.

"With what they've got, they wouldn't know—but it's not the ship's cat," said Peters grimly. He produced a spare pair of seaboots from under his bunk and tossed them over. "Better put these on. You'll need them down there."

———————————◆———————————

A few of the Danish firemen still on deck were rolling up the hoses they'd used, while others, helped by some of the *Velella*'s crew, were transferring equipment back to the tug and fireboat alongside.

Ignoring them all, Sean Peters stalked through the activity to the open lip of number-one hold. He hesitated for only a moment, then, signalling Laird to follow, he began clambering down the iron ladder which led into the hold. Laird followed him, only able to guess at the pain the man must be suffering every time he used his burned hand for support. But Peters went down steadily while the air became heavy and smoky, nipping at their eyes.

Daylight had shrunk to a patch of steel-rimmed blue sky high above by the time they reached the end of a series of ladders and arrived at the bottom gratings. There they found themselves ankle-deep in a lapping residual sludge of water and charred debris, and Laird blessed the borrowed boots he was wearing as he paused and looked around.

It was like being in a dark, menacing cavern, a cavern that reeked of smoke. Water was still dripping everywhere, and a few emergency bulkhead lights cast a dull glow on a shambles of toppled, damaged, or totally destroyed crates and bales. Chemical drums had burst open. What had once been carefully stowed cargo had been reduced to so much water-sodden debris.

Hunter, the young third mate, splashed towards them through the gloom and exchanged a few low-voiced words with Peters. Then he guided them towards the port side, through a maze of partially blocked alleyways, and past more cargo which had been reduced to a tangle of twisted metal and fragmented ash.

A brighter gleam of light appeared ahead. Wading through a final, swampy porridge of burst cartons, they saw two firemen, another of the *Velella*'s officers, and a tall, slim man in civilian clothes standing waiting under the glare of a big battery arc lamp.

"That's Lundgard," Peters muttered in Laird's ear. "Remember, he's all yours."

Sergeant Niels Lundgard was about the same age as Laird. He had long, straight fair hair, a thin face with high cheekbones, and a sad-shaped mouth which twisted a greeting as Peters made brief introductions.

"*Ah, jeg be'r* . . . you might be able to help us, Mr. Laird," said Lundgard, though his voice made it clear that he doubted it. "Let me show you what we found. This way."

The others eased back to let them pass. Then Sean Peters gave a shocked grunt and stopped short. Looking down, Laird felt his stomach tighten as he saw what was lying at their feet.

The charred body of what had been a man lay face upward in the dark sludge of water. Most of the clothes had been burned from his body and only a few wisps of hair remained above the grotesque, crisped mask that had once been his face.

"*Ja*, he is not pretty," said Niels Lundgard apologetically. "I should have warned you, maybe."

Muttering under his breath, Peters took another glance, then stepped back. He'd seen more than he wanted. But Laird stayed, his reactions very different after the first surprise.

It was a long time since he'd first been introduced to the various ways of death. Then, when he thought back, he'd been another Andrew Laird altogether—a young, eagerly brash medical student at a Scottish university. Once a week his class had trooped into an autopsy room for a pathology lecture given by a jovial professor whose hobby was amateur dramatics and who enjoyed being able to produce the unusual in cadavers.

When it came to death by burning, he had insisted on his students being able to recite the standard surgical classifications of burns as if they'd been poetry. Looking down, the list wisped back through Laird's mind.

First-degree surface. Second-degree, vesication. Third, partial destruction of true skin. Fourth, total destruction of true skin. Fifth, into the subcutaneous with involvement of muscular tissue. Sixth, extension in depth with involvement of nerve trunks, serous cavities, and bone.

The man at Laird's feet, his limbs contracted after

death into what pathologists tagged the "pugilistic attitude," had been sixth degree. But as a death it hadn't necessarily been quick.

"Can we move on?" asked Niels Lundgard with an uneasy impatience. "There is something else I want you to see."

They splashed past the horror in the water and Lundgard bent down a little way on. Stooping beside him, Laird saw the twisted remains of a metal cylinder and what had been a clocklike device with melted wiring still attached.

"Maybe you know a little about these things?" queried Lundgard almost lazily.

"Enough." Sensing that he was on trial, Laird ran a finger around a thin white deposit which still clung to the lip of the cylinder. He sampled the powdered residue with the tip of his tongue, then glanced up. "My guess would be a magnesium-based compound—but it's a lab job."

"*Ja.* I would agree." The tall, fair-haired Dane gave a pleased nod, as if they'd reached an understanding, then thumbed over his shoulder towards the dead man. "And my guess would be something went wrong for him."

"It happens," agreed Laird. It would have been a hell of a way to die, alone and in searing agony. But it had happened before and would happen again—any agency file on terrorist activities had its quota of terrorists destroyed by their own bombs.

Sean Peters had been staring at them both, his face still blanked by shock. Now he moved. Nursing his injured arm, he went back through the watery scum and cursed the dead man in a dull voice which echoed flatly in the silence of the hold.

"Chief Officer, we'll presume this to be your missing passenger," said Lundgard laconically. "Olaf Hansen was only travelling to London—from which I'd guess he planned this fire to start much later, when he was safe ashore."

"And when we might have been out in the middle of the damned Atlantic," said Peters tightly.

"*Ja.*" Lundgard rubbed a hand along his chin, then nodded a sober agreement. "But how did he get down here?" Looking around, he pointed up at the open hatch high above. "That way?"

"No," snarled Peters. "The hatches were closed before we sailed. But if he knew his way around the ship—"

"Take it he made sure he did," suggested Lundgard helpfully.

"Then he'd use the lower-deck alleyways," said Peters heavily. "They lead to inspection workways for every hold, with watertight doors—that's the way we came in when we tried to fight the fire."

Laird knew he was sharing the same thought as Niels Lundgard. In the early hours of the morning, with most of the *Velella*'s crew asleep and the duty watch busy, a determined man who knew where he was going would have had an easy enough journey from the passenger cabins to where they were now.

Whatever had gone wrong once he'd got there . . .

"Finished with me, Sergeant?" asked Peters harshly, cutting across the thought.

Lundgard nodded.

"Then I'll get out of here, before I spit on that." Peters glared at the body at their feet. "If anyone aboard knows more about him, you'll hear."

Beckoning his two officers to follow, the *Velella*'s chief officer splashed off through the scummy water. He was making for the rear of the hold, obviously intent on inspecting the alleyway doors.

"Captain Sloan was his friend," said Laird quietly.

"*Ja.* It makes it worse." Niels Lundgard stuck his hands into his jacket pockets, his long face hard to read. "You know what I need most right now? A reason for this fire. Can you give me one, Mr. Laird?"

Laird shook his head. He'd already been thinking, with a rough picture of the *Velella*'s cargo in mind.

"Not in terms of insurance values. It's a normal picture—an ordinary load of cargo, a few items being shipped to London, the bulk of it for the American side." He shrugged. "Once I get a full copy of the loading manifest, that might help."

"Before your insurance claims start arriving?" Lundgard nodded gloomily. "We both have problems."

The Dane paused there, his mouth twisting oddly as if he had been about to add something but had changed his mind. Instead, he looked down at the dead man and grimaced.

"One thing I can almost guarantee," he said dryly. "We will discover he was using a false name and a false passport. But after that—" He shrugged.

"Anything in his cabin that helps?" queried Laird.

"*Nej* . . . nothing. A small suitcase, some overnight things, and enough money to buy him an airline ticket back from London." Lundgard's voice became bleaker. "He could have brought his firebomb aboard in the suitcase— security checks may be strict at airports but things are different at a dockside. Customs squads are more interested in what's coming into a country than what's going out."

Turning, he splashed across to the two firemen still waiting patiently in the background. After speaking to them for a moment, he came back.

"They'll wait here," said Lundgard. "Let's go up on deck and get some air." He looked around with an expression of disgusted resignation. "I'll be back here soon enough once our forensic people arrive."

The smoke-laced atmosphere still nipping his eyes, Laird was happy to agree. They set off, skirting the dead man, leaving the bright glow of the portable arc lamp, and began wading and climbing their way through the cluttered shambles of fire-gutted cargo towards the hatchway ladder.

Laird was in the lead as they rounded a high, partly damaged stack of wooden crates. The steel decking underfoot was slippery and he kept his balance with an effort as he turned to warn Lundgard.

He was a second too late. Lundgard swore as he stumbled and crashed into the crates. Then he gave a hoarse cry of warning as the whole stack shivered, shed fragments of charred wood, then began to topple towards them.

Desperately, Laird hurled himself clear and fell full length in the watery sludge. Behind him, the crates smashed down and loose spars flew in all directions. One clipped his shoulder; then, as the rumble ended, he scrambled up with the sour taste of the sludge in his mouth and his clothes dripping wet.

He couldn't see the Dane. Shouting, the two firemen were pounding across the hold. Quickly Laird clambered over the fallen crates, then stopped.

Lundgard was safe, sitting on the deck with his back against one of the crates. A heavy spar of wood lay across his legs, holding him down, but Lundgard was ignoring it, staring with a near-hypnotised fascination at a stubby black metal cylinder he was cradling in his arms.

"Careful," said Lundgard in a tight, strained voice. He looked up, a lock of his long, fair hair lying across his eyes. "I caught this as it fell."

"Planted among the crates?" asked Laird, his lips suddenly dry.

Lundgard nodded, still nursing the cylinder as if it were the most fragile thing in the world.

"We have a little problem, Mr. Laird," he said slowly, his voice hoarse. "The timer is still working. I can hear it ticking."

The two firemen were trying to crowd in. Fiercely, Laird waved them back and tried to think. The timer section of the firebomb was sealed in a casing of what looked like light-gauge tin. He could see the lugs of a simple starter screw. But the cylinder had already suffered a minor roasting, even if the full heat of the blaze caused by its twin hadn't reached it. The soaking that had followed when the hold was flooded could have caused its own unpredictable complications.

The thing in Lundgard's arms wasn't for playing with. Beads of sweat forming on the Dane's forehead showed that he knew it, too.

Turning to the watching firemen, Laird beckoned them in and had them lift the spar of wood trapping Lundgard's legs. They did the job with nervous care, then strayed back again—and he couldn't blame them. Anxiously, Lundgard moved his legs a little, flexed his ankles, then gave a sigh of relief.

"Okay," he reported, and forced a grin. "Maybe if you took our problem for a moment—"

Laird wiped his hands dry on his shirt, took the black cylinder from him, and felt the slow ticking of the timer as he held the cold metal against his chest. Lundgard hauled himself upright slowly, tried a couple of hobbling steps, winced a little, but nodded.

"I'll manage. We want rid of that thing quick, right?"

"Damned quick," agreed Laird fervently.

"Up the ladder and over the side." Lundgard looked up at the long stretch of runged ladder which led to the main deck above, took a deep breath, and tried another hobbling step. "*Ja.* I can make it. This is only bruising."

"Like hell you can," said Laird bleakly. "You'd need both hands to hang on—are you planning on carrying Our Problem in your teeth or something?"

Lundgard scowled. "It's my job as a police officer."

"So you're a sergeant," said Laird wearily. "Look, all that worries me is that if you fell with the damned thing I'd be the idiot underneath."

Lundgard glared at him for a moment, tried another couple of shuffling steps, then sighed.

"It's still ticking," said Laird pointedly. "Get the hell out of my way, will you?"

Reluctantly, Lundgard obeyed. The two firemen had already increased their distance.

Andrew Laird walked the rest of the way to the ladder as if the deck were paved with eggshells. Then he eased the firebomb until it was in the crook of his left arm, locked his other arm around the ladder, and started upward.

He moved slowly, concentrating on every rung, the ticking from the cylinder's timing mechanism almost overtaken by the pounding of his heart. Twice a fractional error in the way he climbed jarred the bomb against the ladder—and each time he froze, ready for a sunburst of fury to erupt.

It seemed a long, long time before he reached the top of the ladder and the lip of the hatchway. He hauled himself out onto the deck, yelled a warning to a group of *Velella* crewmen who were standing near, then carried the firebomb over towards the rail. It was still ticking as he shifted the cylinder over to his right hand, then hurled it overarm in a curving arc which sent it out and far away from the hull.

The black cylinder hit the sea with a splash which became a flat explosion. As spray drenched up, Laird saw a momentary red eruption of flame; then it was gone as the cylinder sank. A thin, furious trail of bubbles marked its path down towards the bottom of the Øresund Strait.

He rested his hands on the rail, and they were shaking. The *Velella*'s crewmen were running over, staring over the side, though there was nothing left for them to see. Then he heard slow footsteps behind him, turned, and somehow wasn't surprised as Lundgard limped over to join him at the rail.

"A long climb," said the Dane mildly.

"Long enough, Sergeant," agreed Laird.

Pensively, Lundgard looked himself up and down, then considered Laird. Their clothes were equally soaked and filthy from the watery scum of the hold. As he caught Laird's eye, his long, raw-boned face shaped a grin.

"My friends call me Niels—friends and people I decide I don't mind having to work with," said the Dane. *"Ja,* it should be interesting having to work with an Englishman."

"Then get it right at the start," said Laird dryly. "I'm a Scot. There's a difference."

"I know," said Lundgard seriously. "My ancestors were Vikings—we used to visit Scotland a lot."

Laird couldn't answer that one.

CHAPTER TWO

A ten-minute soak under a hot shower followed by a brief, almost agonising needle blast of cold water left Andrew Laird feeling clean again. He rubbed himself down with a towel, then, still naked, walked across his hotel bedroom to the small refrigerator located near the bed. Taking out a can of beer, he tore off the ring pull. After a long gulp from the can, he went over to the window.

From ten storeys up, he looked out at the warm, sunlit evening. It was five o'clock, the Edelstenen Hotel was located close to the centre of Copenhagen, and on the road down below, the city's homeward rush-hour traffic was beginning to build up. Danish style, scores of pedal cyclists were competing with cars and busses while small, snarling motorcycles carved a way through them all.

Laird had been in Copenhagen before, but it was the first time he'd stayed at the Edelstenen; Clanmore's local agent, Per Jensen, had made the booking. It was the kind of hotel where a Scandinavian version of chrome and plastic comfort was tailored to cater to visiting business traffic. Though when Laird had returned from the *Velella* the front lobby reception had made it clear that guests weren't meant to show up looking and smelling as if they'd crawled out of a sewer.

He grinned at the memory, rested his muscular, heavily tattooed arms on the window ledge, and spent a moment longer looking out at the view. Beyond the road was a narrow strip of blue water, an inland lake, with its quota of small pleasure boats being rowed around. Then the city began again, a mixture of domes and spires and red tile roofs with the occasional intrusion of a modern high-rise glass-and-concrete office block.

Turning away, Laird went over to the chair where he'd laid out a change of clothing from his suitcase. His damp and dirty suit was already in one of the hotel laundry bags, waiting to be collected. Still sipping the beer, he put on a cream-coloured shirt and grey whipcord slacks; then, barefoot, took the can over to the bed and sprawled back on the covers.

There was work lying waiting for him. Before he'd left the *Velella* he'd collected a duplicate of her loading manifest and a copy of her passenger list. They thickened out the miserably thin information file he'd brought from London but he had a gloomy feeling of certainty that it still represented only a start to a lot of trouble ahead.

The thought sparked another. Reaching for the telephone on the bedside table, he dialled Per Jensen's number. The Clanmore local agent operated from a small office in Copenhagen's business section. Laird knew that he should have contacted the man earlier, except Jensen wasn't one of his favourite people—and he had a feeling that Jensen felt much the same way about him.

The phone at Jensen's office was answered straight away and the man's distinctive, high-pitched voice gave a squeak of feigned pleasure as soon as Laird spoke.

"Five minutes more and you would have missed me, Andrew." Jensen made it sound like tragedy averted. "I would have left for home. *Hvordan har De det* . . . how are you?"

"Still surviving." Laird forestalled the inevitable. "Sorry I can't see you tonight—I've got to go out. But I'll look around at your office tomorrow."

"I might have come to the Edelstenen and let you buy me a drink," said Jensen, and made a throat-clearing noise. "All right, tomorrow. But I have a cable here for you, a message from London."

"Are they complaining already?" asked Laird wearily.

"*Nej* . . . not yet." Jensen giggled a little. "It isn't too important. Your head office just confirmed that you've been appointed to act for all insurance companies who have an interest in the *Velella* or her cargo." He paused, then added slyly, "There's also a mention that my agency will qualify for special payment if we are involved in extra work. So—ah—"

"So you're ready to earn it?" Laird kept his manner neutral but gave the telephone mouthpiece a sardonic grin. Jensen was fat and middle-aged, never spent money if someone else might do it, and was reputed to have some strange friends around Copenhagen—though he also had a busty blond wife tucked away in a suburb, where she probably cost less to run than a housekeeper. But Jensen knew the insurance game, which was why Clanmore kept him on. "All right, how are your contacts with the harbour police?"

"Excellent," declared Jensen modestly. "I know, for instance, that the *Velella* will not dock till tomorrow. The police are insisting on a full search, just in case there is a third firebomb aboard—"

"You've got contacts," agreed Laird, cutting the man short. "What I need from you right now is a firm line on anything the harbour police are saying or doing about that ship. If they turn up any surprises, call me."

He said goodbye, replaced the receiver, and drank a little more of the beer. The London cable simply confirmed what he'd suspected from the moment he'd flown out. It had been inevitable. Clanmore Alliance had a sixty-per-cent share of the *Velella*'s hull-and-machinery risk cover and a computer-estimated thirty-per-cent share of her cargo insurance.

Andrew Laird couldn't even guess at the total number of insurance firms that might be involved. When a ship sailed, the marine-insurance world still used the old-fashioned term "the adventure" to describe the voyage ahead. They took shares in the risk, spreading the basic gamble around in a way that kept the dreaded accountants happy.

Another pattern could begin when an "adventure" became major trouble. The firm with the biggest stake would act for all in the early stages, keeping down cost and confusion.

That was the way it was now, and he'd been left on the sharp end. Shrugging, Laird reached for the *Velella* file again. As he opened it, a crumpled slip of paper fell out and landed on the bedcover. He picked it up, saw the scribble in Sean Peters' handwriting, and remembered the girl the chief officer had asked him to contact. "Karen Leslie, c/o Hotel Brochen"—whatever she might be like, she was Captain Sloan's niece, Sloan was dead, and she had been a fellow passenger of the man directly responsible.

He picked up the telephone again, dialled the number Peters had written, and asked for Karen Leslie when the Hotel Brochen switchboard answered. The operator left him holding for a few seconds, then came back on the line. Karen Leslie was out, but she had left word she'd return in an hour.

He hung up, settled back with his beer and the *Velella*

file, and began reading. Even with the cool taste of the beer to lubricate his mind it was a dull task. The cargo manifest sheets came down to column after column of the kind of unglamorous freight which formed the livelihood of most of the ships on the Atlantic run.

Five hundred tons of dried milk in the aft holds was being shipped to London, where there was other cargo waiting. Machinery, sugar, and textiles were the start of the list for Boston. Then there were pharmaceutical products, furniture from a couple of Danish manufacturers, china plate, and scores of smaller consignments . . . all to be loaded according to a plan on which any ship's stability and safety depended.

He hadn't expected much in the high-value, low-bulk category and there wasn't. The big jets of the air-freight lines had syphoned that kind of traffic away from the sea. The *Velella*'s cargo was ordinary, at least on paper. No high-risk insurance items, no politically awkward military shipments or anything else likely to attract a firebomb aimed either at fraud or at protest . . .

Laird reached for his beer again. The can was empty, and he lit another cigarette instead, then lay back, watching the way the evening sunlight poured in through his window and half listening to the muffled rumble of the traffic outside.

He was thinking of the insurance tangle one or two cargo owners were going to find ahead, glad he wouldn't have to sort that out. A lot would depend on the kind of cover they'd taken, but for some, who had tried to cut corners and costs, Paragraph H. 24 in a few policies might be an unpleasant surprise. It excluded any claim for loss which resulted from "Any person acting maliciously or from a political motive."

Small print in marine insurance held its surprises for

the unwary—and made the final verdict reached by the Danish police important in more ways than one.

The telephone began ringing. Stretching over for the receiver, Laird propped it lazily against his shoulder and answered.

"God aften, Mr. Laird," said a precise, distinctly Scandinavian voice. "My name is Vassen—Professor Harald Vassen. A former student of mine, Sergeant Lundgard of the harbour police, suggested you might help me."

"If I can, I'll try," said Laird cautiously, puzzled.

"Good." His caller sounded relieved. "Lundgard tells me you are in Copenhagen to deal with insurance aspects in the *Velella* fire. I—ah—have an interest in part of her cargo."

"Claims aren't my department right now, Professor." Sitting up, Laird nursed the phone nearer his ear, hoping his thoughts of a moment earlier weren't coming to life. "Your local agent is the man to contact. But I'd wait—only the cargo in the for'ard holds was damaged."

"My shipment was totally destroyed," snapped Vassen. "Lundgard checked."

"Then it depends on the kind of insurance cover you had—" began Laird.

"Full cover was arranged, and I intend following your commercial routine," said Vassen stiffly. "But Lundgard was told something which puzzles me, something he thought you could explain."

"I'll try." Laird mentally cursed the tall, fair, sad-faced Dane. "Go on."

"Thank you." He heard a sniff. "One of the *Velella's* officers suggested that cargo loss might be classified as general average. Unfortunately, Lundgard didn't have a chance to ask what that meant—I believe he discovered a dead man or that there was some similar interruption."

"Like you said, there was an interruption," agreed Laird woodenly.

"And this 'general average'?" insisted Vassen. "Does it mean difficulties?"

"No, it's just a piece of insurance jargon," soothed Laird. "Forget about it, Professor. Nothing is decided yet, and general average wouldn't materially affect your claim anyway." He chuckled sympathetically. "If you want an easy definition, it means that people whose property was also on the *Velella* but wasn't damaged may pay for part of your loss. But it's something that all happens between insurance offices, bookkeeping entries . . . like knock-for-knock agreements in car insurance."

"Thank you, I'm grateful." Vassen's voice lost a little of its abruptness over the line. "I—well, I distrust the unknown."

"That's how my company make a living." Laird's curiosity won. "What were you shipping out, Professor—university equipment?"

"Didn't Lundgard tell you?" Vassen sounded surprised. "A full-scale replica Viking longship, insured for three hundred thousand Danish kroner during shipment, then an equivalent seventy thousand American dollars after that."

"You mean it was going on some kind of tour?" queried Laird.

"*Ja* . . . though that is a crude description." The voice in his ear frosted for a moment. "Lundgard can explain. He is one of our oarsmen—and we have another longship, fortunately. Viking spirit and Viking thrust will achieve the rest, Mr. Laird."

The line went dead. Laird blinked, put down the receiver slowly, then got hold of the manifest sheets again and checked them through in disbelief.

But what had to be the longship was there, hidden away after a large consignment of electric motors and unromantically listed as "sectional sports boat and associated equipment, eight crates." Niels Lundgard had been holding out, he decided wryly. Even so, it wasn't major. A three-hundred-thousand-kroner claim could be classed as lightweight compared with some that would be coming in.

Suddenly Laird realised that the last time he'd eaten was at noon, on the flight coming over, and he felt hungry. Getting up, he finished dressing and a reminiscent twitch of a grin touched his lips as he fastened his shirt cuffs over the tattoo marks on his arms. A stylised Chinese dragon clawed rampant on his left arm. The foul anchor on the other arm had a decorative chain which led up towards his biceps.

They were permanent reminders of Hong Kong. The same night he'd acquired them he'd ended up with a broken nose and a feeling of relief that he'd got back aboard ship. But that had been a long time ago, when he was trying to find a new Andrew Laird, having just lost the old one . . . the Andrew Laird, sheep farmer's son from the Scottish Highlands, who had blown his final examinations at medical school after being in line for the class gold medal.

There were no second chances when part of the reason for a student coming unstuck amounted to refusing to go on just watching a woman suffering in a way which could have only one drawn-out ending. The woman had been his mother, but that, he'd been told almost sympathetically, was incidental. In medicine the crime was one of being caught— even if the evidence fell short of any kind of police action.

Afterwards, he had wanted away from people who knew him and the Merchant Navy had been an escape route. Deep-sea at first, as a deck hand . . . that had included Hong Kong. Then, as the new Andrew Laird started to emerge, he'd been a radio operator on an oceangoing salvage tug, and wanted nothing more—for a time, at any rate.

Laird heard a knock at his room door. A maid came in and collected his discarded suit for cleaning. Once she'd gone, he pulled on a grey whipcord jacket which matched his slacks, checked his pockets, added a pack of cigarettes from the duty-free carton he'd bought on the plane, then took the elevator down to the lobby.

The Edelstenen's desk clerk still treated him with a certain disdain but in a couple of minutes he'd arranged to hire a self-drive car. Then Laird wandered through to the hotel coffee shop, selected a herring salad *smørrebrod* and a cup of strong dark coffee, and took them over to a table.

By the time he'd finished eating, the self-drive car was waiting at the kerb outside. It was a small, boxy two-door Simca, dark blue in colour—unimpressive to look at but a car which he knew from experience could be thrashed flat out for hours on end yet prove itself equally at ease dawdling through traffic. He signed for the keys, got directions to the Hotel Brochen, checked them against a town map that was in the Simca's glove box, then started the engine and set the little car moving out into the traffic.

His route took him south, past more of central Copenhagen's little boating lakes, then down a broad street lined with department stores. Skirting the vast, busy Town Hall Square with its bronze statues and lofty towers, the Simca was held at traffic lights while a flood of pedestrians crossed. Once the lights changed, he squeezed around a corner at the same time as a two-unit streetcar, had to brake hard as a truck cut in just ahead, and heard a squeal of tyres and brakes from a motorcyclist just on his tail.

The traffic was easier once he got into Hans Christian Andersen Boulevard, but he had to turn off again just before a bridge over a waterway. The new road stayed with

the waterfront while the Simca kept pace with tourist
launches and passed slow-moving tugs towing strings of
barges. The motorcyclist was still with him, but roared
away as he slowed for the sidestreet where the Hotel Brochen was located.

There was parking space outside the hotel. Leaving
the car, he glanced briefly at the Brochen's mellow brick-
work, then went into its cool, dark, old-fashioned lobby. A
massive, elderly woman behind the reception desk glared at
him suspiciously as he asked for Karen Leslie and gave his
name.

A couple of minutes passed and the woman kept him
under surveillance. Then an antique elevator grunted down
from an upper floor and its door coughed open. The sole
passenger, a girl wearing beige trousers and a pastel green
blouse, stepped out and came towards him.

"Mr. Laird?" she asked in a quiet, pleasant voice. "I'm
Karen Leslie—I had word you'd be coming."

"Good. That helps." He moistened his lips, knowing
he was staring at her and that there was nothing he could do
about it. Then, as Laird recovered from the initial shock
and his mind went somersaulting back in time, he forced a
smile. "Glad to meet you."

Karen Leslie was tall and slim and in her twenties.
She had a small, high bust, green eyes, an attractive fine-
boned face, and short, glinting copper hair. Her walk was
like the rest of her personality, easy and confident.

Most men would have reacted to her. But Andrew
Laird felt numbed, for Karen Leslie resembled so closely
another girl he'd known.

Her name was Maureen. She was the reason why he'd
quit the sea and started in the marine-insurance game—
she'd made it plain she only wanted a husband who would
be around. He'd used his Merchant Navy discharge pay to

buy the engagement ring—and three months later she'd
pawned it for an air ticket to Canada, going off with a man
he hadn't known existed.

Laird had received the pawn ticket as a goodbye message.

Karen Leslie was still waiting, beginning to look
slightly puzzled.

"Sorry." Laird forced the ghost out of his mind.
"You're very like someone I used to know. Who told you
about me?"

"Sergeant Lundgard," she explained. "I had to go to
his office to give a statement. Then when I got back to the
hotel there was a message to say you'd telephoned."

Lundgard wasn't wasting time, decided Laird. He saw
that the woman at the reception desk was still eyeing them
with a suspicious interest.

"I could buy you a drink," he suggested. "Things
might be more private that way."

The hotel cocktail bar was down the corridor, a small,
drab, almost deserted place. They took a corner table, the
girl ordered a cognac, and Laird settled for whisky. Their
drinks came quickly and once he'd been paid the waiter
ambled back to resume reading a newspaper.

"*Skaal,*" said Laird, raising his glass.

Karen Leslie nodded and barely touched her drink
with her lips. Watching her, Laird decided there were subtle
differences. Maureen's hair was darker and she'd parted it
another way. Karen Leslie's mouth was wider, her lips nar-
rower—he stopped there, before it became a catalogue.

"Why did you choose this hotel?" he asked, for something to say.

"I stayed here a couple of nights till I could go aboard
the *Velella.*" She laid down her glass, her green eyes serious.
"Now, what is it you really want, Mr. Laird?"

Laird shrugged. "In the beginning, I promised a red-haired first mate out of Liverpool that I'd look you up. He was worried about you—mother-hen style."

"Sean Peters." Her face softened into a smile. "I should have guessed."

"You'll probably see him tomorrow. He thought he'd get the *Velella* docked by tonight, but that's been delayed."

"Sergeant Lundgard told me." Her lips tightened for a moment. "Why do you think this all happened to—well, why the *Velella?*"

Laird shrugged. "That's what a lot of people want to find out." He paused. "I know this thing is personal to you—that Captain Sloan was your uncle. From what I've heard, I'm sorry I never met him."

"He was pretty much a stranger to me too. I'm glad of that now." She fumbled with her handbag and took out a cigarette. Laird gave her a light and watched for a moment as she drew on the smoke.

"Tell me about him," he suggested.

"He was really my mother's cousin," she said slowly. "His family left England when he was a child, settled in Australia, and then it was the usual 'distant relative' thing— one or two letters a year and a gift each Christmas. But he became my 'sailor uncle'—he visited us a couple of times when his ship touched Britain and he had leave."

"How did it happen you were sailing to Boston with him?" asked Laird, sipping his drink. From the raw taste of the whisky, he wished he'd checked the bottle.

"I've a job waiting out there as a research assistant— laboratory work. I'm a qualified chemist." Karen Leslie frowned at the cigarette between her fingers. "I'd been working in Paris for a spell and I'd written to him a couple of times, so I knew his ship was on the Copenhagen–Boston run. I wrote and told him about the Boston job and he wrote back and suggested I take the sea trip with him on the *Velella*." Her eyes clouded. "I liked the idea—I thought it would be a holiday."

"What will you do now?" asked Laird sympathetically.

"Wait here a few days. The police think it might help and—well, we've still relatives in Australia. There will be arrangements to be made." Her mouth tightened. "It was bad enough when I thought that fire was an accident. But now—"

"That's what I want to talk about," said Laird quietly. "What you heard and what you saw before the fire. I've my own job to do, Karen."

"You mean you want to hear about this man who called himself Olaf Hansen."

He nodded. "You met him?"

"He was in the cabin next to mine." She toyed with her drink again, a new bitterness in her voice. "We met on deck after the *Velella* sailed and talked for a spell. Then later on we shared a table when we ate. It just happened that way— none of the other passengers were around and my uncle was still on the bridge."

"The man we found was pretty badly burned," said Laird, making it a deliberate understatement. "How would you describe Hansen?"

She shrugged. "Young, reasonably good-looking, dark-haired—he was about medium height and slightly plump. Sergeant Lundgard had me try to make up an Identikit picture of him but I wouldn't say it was very good."

"It'll help, whatever it's like. What did he talk about?"

"The usual things, I suppose. About the weather, about being at sea—he said he always felt nervous in aircraft so he was giving the ship way to England a try." She gave a small, tight, humourless laugh. "I still thought he seemed nervous—but I didn't guess the reason."

He nodded. "Anything else, Karen?"

She thought about it. "I know he was the last passenger to come aboard. A taxi dropped him off at the dockside not long before we sailed. And he told me he was going on a selling trip to London for an engineering firm—but he was vague about it." A sudden frown creased her forehead. "There was one other thing—I'd forgotten about it till now. When I told him I'd be working in Boston—"

"Well?"

"He was interested. He said he might be there soon, that he might have to fly over on a business trip."

It was Laird's turn to frown. "Did he say when?"

"No." Karen Leslie stifled the start of a yawn and grimaced apologetically. "Sorry—I'm not particularly bright company right now. Looking back, it's like I spent half of last night standing around in a lifejacket."

"You could use some sleep." For the first time, he really saw the tiredness in her eyes. "I've got to go anyway—I want another talk with Lundgard, then I've a first report to draft for London."

"He told me he'd be at the harbour police office most of the night." She paused. "Before you go, tell me something."

"If I can."

She smiled a little. "Who was the girl, the one you thought I looked like?"

Laird grinned and finished his drink. "Just someone I used to know."

"Just someone?" She raised a quizzical eyebrow.

He nodded and got to his feet. "Get that sleep you need. I'd like to come back tomorrow, sometime."

"Do that." She stubbed out her cigarette and glanced around. "I won't be doing much."

She left the bar with him and they walked together

through the lobby of the hotel. The fat woman behind the reception desk looked up as they passed, then ignored them.

"They call Copenhagen the fairy-tale city," said Laird sadly. "I suppose they've got to have a few witches on the fringe."

Karen Leslie laughed, said goodnight as they reached the door, and went back towards the elevator while Laird headed out to his car.

Once he had the Simca back on the main road, Laird followed the waterfront route north for a short spell. Then the road eased inland, still heading north, past the rococo splendour of the Amalienbourg Palace, where tourists were already clustering for the next changing of the toy-soldierlike Royal Guard, then along the fringe of the old star-shaped Kastellet citadel with its green parkland and water moats.

Dusk came late in Scandinavian latitudes—late and slowly. The evening was still bright, the traffic only moderate, and Laird was driving at an easy pace when a casual, routine glance at the car's rear mirror made him frown and come alert again.

A motorcyclist was travelling about half a dozen vehicles back, matching Laird's car speed. The figure wore black leathers and a black crash helmet. Maybe he had a hundred twins in terms of outfit among Copenhagen's motorcycling population, but there was something familiar about the set of the rider's shoulders and the way he held his head.

Deliberately, Laird slowed a little. The motorcyclist also slowed, keeping the same gap. Laird kept his eyes on the rear mirror for another short spell, then swore softly. It

had to be the same rider he'd noticed when he'd driven to
meet Karen Leslie at the Hotel Brochen.

To make sure, Laird gently increased his speed again
and overtook a couple of cars. The rider behind immediately matched the movement, maintaining the distance.
Laird shrugged, used the dashboard lighter to light a cigarette, and decided that for the moment the best thing to do
was ignore the shadow.

Copenhagen's dockland came up, heavy container
trucks fattening out the traffic while tall cranes, the bright
upper decks and masts of ships, and the bulk of massive
grain elevators took over on the seaward side.

Laird knew where he was heading but he still had to
watch for the turnoff. It came up, he steered the Simca
down the right-hand branch of a fork in the road, bounced
the car over a couple of railroad-level crossings with the
motorcyclist now a shade farther back, then saw the harbour *politistationen* just ahead.

He pulled the car into the kerb outside, stopped, and
checked his mirror again. The rider had vanished and could
be anywhere in the warren of sidestreets and alleys which
lay all around. When Laird climbed out of the car the only
people in sight were a group of foreign seamen making a
cheerful way along the street from some ship to some bar.

The *politistationen* was small, a suboffice catering for
just a section of Copenhagen's vast dockland. Inside, Laird
spoke to a constable who wore the Danish force's summer
rig of open-necked, short-sleeved shirt, dark slacks, and for-
age cap. The constable had a pistol holstered at his waist,
and two more uniformed men exchanging gossip at a coffee
machine behind him had machine pistols slung over their
shoulders.

Directed through to the detective section, Laird discovered Niels Lundgard alone in a small, cluttered office.

The tall, fair-haired sergeant was sitting at a desk with his feet up and had a telephone at his ear. Lundgard's long, sad face crinkled into a grin of welcome and he waved Laird into a chair. Then, finishing the call quickly, he hung up.

"*Hvordan* . . . how are things, Andrew?" he asked.

"Reasonable," said Laird dryly. "But I'd like to know why I've picked up a tail. Is he one of your people?"

"*Nej*." Lundgard blinked his surprise. "You're sure?"

Laird nodded. "He's on a motorcycle and wearing black leathers. He faded away just before I stopped outside."

"If he was one of our boys, you wouldn't have spotted him. It's a rule we have." Lundgard rubbed a hand along his chin. "Why you? It doesn't make much sense." He began to reach for the telephone again. "I can make an arrangement—"

"No, leave him." Laird pushed his hand away from the telephone. "He might be more useful the way he is."

"If you want it that way," said Lundgard slowly. "But if it happens again—"

"I'll let you know," promised Laird.

"Good." The Dane swept some of the papers on his desk into a file, then dumped the file into a drawer. "Did you meet Karen Leslie?"

"Yes."

Lundgard sighed. "A girl to remember. I—ah—may have to see her again."

"That makes two of us," said Laird dryly.

Lundgard grinned. "What else happened to you?"

"Your Professor Vassen telephoned." Laird eyed him stonily.

"*Ja*, I suggested that." Lundgard brought his feet down off the desk and looked slightly uneasy. "We were both puzzled by this term 'general average.'"

"I explained it to him. When there's a situation when some of the freight aboard a ship is sacrificed to save the ship and the rest of her cargo, the people who didn't lose take a share in footing the bill—or their insurance companies do." Laird knew he'd have been damned by any insurance lawyer for that kind of simplicity, but it was near enough to basic truth. "The *Velella* was saved because those for'ard holds were flooded."

"So it could be claimed that some of the cargo in those holds was deliberately destroyed?" Lundgard still looked puzzled. "Does it matter?"

"Only to the insurance companies." Laird got up, crossed over to a wall-mounted watercooler, and came back sipping at a paper cup. "Why didn't you tell me about this mock-up Viking boat?"

"At the time, we had other things to worry about." Lundgard's thin face showed a touch of embarrassment. "Did Professor Vassen explain—?"

"He was too busy jumping up and down about whether the insurance would pay out," said Laird. "He left that to you. How important is he, anyway?"

"One of the five greatest living authorities on Viking history and culture." Niels Lundgard's voice held considerable respect.

"What culture?" asked Laird with a touch of malice. "I thought they were just a hairy heavy mob who retired into the beer commercials."

Lundgard swore at him good-humouredly. "Harald Vassen could prove it differently, Andrew. He happens to have one of the world's finest collections of Viking relics. Haven't you heard of the Vassen Trust Collection?"

Laird shook his head and the Dane sighed.

"It is important enough to have gone on exhibition in top museums and galleries throughout Europe, my friend.

Now he is taking it out to America for the first time. It is being flown out to Boston next month, then on to New York—and don't ask me how much it is worth. The only answer I could give is 'priceless.'"

"So where does this longship fit in?" asked Laird patiently. "He said you helped crew it."

"*Ja.*" Lundgard unfastened a couple of shirt buttons, reached inside, and brought out a medallion which hung around his neck on a long leather thong. "I'm a member of a rowing club he runs. This is our badge."

Going over, Laird examined the medallion. Glinting in the light, the bright metal carried the emblem of a Viking longship, her long banks of oars reaching out to bite the water.

"But how does it tie in with his exhibitions?"

"We take out a replica of an old longship, one built in sections that bolt together." Lundgard carefully tucked the medallion away again and fastened the shirt buttons. "The exhibitions are always in a city which is a seaport or has a river. Then, if you have a Viking longship sailing around, manned by a full crew in Viking dress—"

"Your professor has the media coverage made." Laird finished it for him, his respect for Harald Vassen increasing. "Who foots the bills?"

"The Vassen Trust." Lundgard stroked his chin. "Forty of us were to fly out to Boston in three weeks time, to man the oars. After the fire, I had thought it was goodbye to that trip—but Professor Vassen says he can still get another boat out in time."

"Good luck to him," said Laird absently. He emptied the paper cup and tossed it into Lundgard's wastebasket. "What's the latest from the *Velella?*"

"Everything under control, the aft holds searched, and Chief Officer Peters says he'll have her docked here for breakfast tomorrow." Lundgard scowled. "I wish things were as good all around. Our firebomb maniac Olaf Hansen was a fake."

"That shouldn't have been too much of a surprise," mused Laird.

"The passport he used was forged, the business address he gave doesn't exist, he bought his ticket for cash three days ago." Lundgard slapped the flat of his hand on the desk. *"Faerdig . . .* it finishes there."

"But it stays your case?"

Lundgard nodded sadly. "My inspector is on vacation, headquarters say they are short-staffed and can't spare anyone. Short-staffed?" Indignantly, he got up and crossed over to a wall map of Copenhagen's dockland, gesturing its length. "Here's what the harbour division has to deal with— sixty kilometres of quays and docks, anything up to three hundred and fifty ships in harbour, leaving harbour or coming in. Bring the average headquarters man down here and he'd have a nervous breakdown within the hour!"

"You've got problems." Laird nodded sympathetically, wondering if there was a police force anywhere that didn't have the same jaundiced view of its headquarters staff. "Karen Leslie says she made up an Identikit picture of Hansen. Could I see it?"

"Ja." The Dane went back to his desk, raked around it for a moment, then tossed the Identikit picture across. "Olaf Hansen—we might as well call him that for convenience."

The face Karen Leslie had built from the Identikit selections stared up at Laird. It was a young man's face. He had dark, short, straight hair, and round, slightly sullen features, with a small mouth.

"Weight maybe sixty-five kilos—say one hundred forty pounds, medium height, medium build." Lundgard came around and scowled down at the picture. "I have sent out copies to every police station in case someone knows him. Though"—he stopped and rubbed his jaw unhappily—"every time I look at that face I tell myself I should know him. That maybe I do."

"How about the other passengers who were aboard?" queried Laird.

"Seen and ruled out," said Lundgard briefly. "They noticed him, that's all. Before you ask, the other passenger for London was an elderly American schoolteacher—not the firebomb type."

The office door opened and a woman looked in. An angular blonde in her early thirties, she had the bluest pair of eyes Laird could remember and wore a faded blue denim jacket over a grey shirt and trousers. Seeing Laird, she stopped and glanced at Lundgard.

"*Kom ind* . . . come in, Nina," invited Lundgard. "This is Andrew Laird, the man from London I talked about." He glanced slyly at Laird as the blonde walked in and let the door swing shut behind her. "Andrew, meet our Sergeant Kristensen—blue-eyed innocence and a heart of steel."

Sergeant Kristensen smiled slightly at Laird, then shook her head at Lundgard's unspoken question.

"*Nej*, no luck, Niels," she said in a surprisingly quiet voice. "Not yet, anyway."

She went past them and dumped a bulky leather shoulderbag in another of the desks. Sitting on the desk, she picked up a telephone and dialled a number, totally ignoring them.

"We want to find the taxi that brought Hansen to the docks when he boarded the *Velella*," explained Lundgard. "If we can trace back to where he came from, it might be a start point."

"There's also how he knew his way around the ship so well," mused Laird.

Lundgard shrugged. "It's an ordinary enough layout, *min ven*. But if he did have help aboard from any of the crew—well, that's another little job for our Nina." He glanced over, saw that the blonde was now talking on the telephone, and murmured, "Don't let the blue eyes deceive you. There are times I'm glad I have six months' seniority as sergeant."

He stopped there as the phone on his own desk rang. Answering it, Lundgard listened and scribbled some quick notes with a pencil. Finally, his long face suddenly bleak, he muttered his thanks and hung up.

"Headquarters," he said shortly for Laird's benefit. Bringing out a battered pack of cigarettes, he took one, then as an afterthought flicked another across to Laird. He waited until they shared a light, then took a long draw of smoke and let it out with a sigh. "*Ja*, life is full of little surprises."

"Trouble?" asked Laird.

Lundgard nodded. Behind them, Sergeant Kristensen had finished her telephone call and was listening.

"Remember you saw what was left of the detonator on that first firebomb, the one that killed Hansen?" asked Lundgard wearily.

"It looked usual enough. What about it?"

Laird waited.

"Our forensic people say the timing mechanism had been deliberately altered." Lundgard chewed his lip. "The thing was wired to explode the moment the activating switch was moved."

A vision of the grotesque, crisped body in the *Velella*'s fire-gutted hold came unbidden into Laird's mind and he felt a moment's cold revulsion. He glanced around at Sergeant Kristensen. She was still listening, but she had taken a mirror and lipstick from her handbag and was slowly repairing her light makeup.

It meant there had been someone else behind Hansen. Someone ruthless enough to have decided that the creature he had used would not be allowed to exist afterwards as any kind of risk. He frowned, puzzled about something else. The other firebomb's timer couldn't have been tampered with—but if Hansen had expected to plant two, that was maybe reasonable enough.

One had been enough to guarantee that Hansen would die like a human torch.

"They want me at headquarters." Lundgard glanced at his desk. "I have a few things to do first—"

"It's time I left anyway." Laird stubbed his cigarette in an ashtray and took a first step towards the door.

"Andrew—" Lundgard stopped him. "If your motorcyclist friend appears again, I need to know." He grimaced. "If this remains my case, that is."

"I'll tell you," promised Laird.

The Dane nodded, then gave a wry smile. "Another thing—I had forgotten it. Professor Vassen thought you might like to see our Viking longship crew in action."

Laird blinked a little. "When?"

"Early tomorrow morning, around seven o'clock—that way, it is before most of the club have to start work. We've a practice row at Tostig—it's a fishing village on the coast, about thirty kilometres north of here." Lundgard gestured apologetically. "You could meet him there. I don't know if I can make it, but I'll try."

"Has this bunch of athletic delinquents got a name?" queried Laird.

Lundgard looked slightly sheepish. "We call ourselves the Berserkers."

"Do you, now?" Laird grinned, remembering a fragment of his schoolboy history lessons. "The wildest of the lot in the Viking league, weren't they? Scared the hell out of the rest of Europe every time they sailed?"

"*Ja,* Mr. Laird." Sergeant Kristensen laid down her lipstick and considered Lundgard sardonically. "There was even a prayer for protection from them—'From the fury of the Northmen, deliver us, Oh Lord.'"

"Not anymore," said Lundgard sadly, and sighed. "Today, we have too many problems with our women."

CHAPTER THREE

Dusk had already greyed over the waterfront as Andrew Laird drove the rented Simca away from the police station. What he'd expected soon happened. The same motorcyclist made his appearance in the rear-view mirror before the car reached the main road and from then on it became the pattern as before. The black-clad rider slotted into the citybound traffic a few vehicles back and stayed there with a dogged patience.

As the sky continued to dull, Laird switched on the Simca's driving lights. The streetlamps came on and neon shop signs formed a bright avenue ahead in the gathering twilight.

Checking his mirror, Laird saw the motorcycle's headlight still showing the same distance to the rear. Then an idea came to him, startling in simplicity if he could achieve it.

"Why not?" he heard himself say aloud. "The hell with him—"

But it had to be timed carefully. He tried to remember more detail of the route he'd travelled on the outward trip, let a couple of lights-controlled junctions pass, then chose the next one as it appeared ahead.

Slowing, he allowed a few vehicles to overtake him

and made sure the motorcycle was still hanging back. The traffic lights were at green, then as the Simca drew nearer they started to change.

Laird slammed the Simca's gear change straight down from top to second and rammed the accelerator to the floor. The little car clawed forward, engine screaming, and raced across the junction with the traffic light at red against it, and the other, newly released stream of vehicles starting to move.

Horns hooted and brakes squealed. But he was through—and he grinned as he glanced in the mirror and saw the motorcycle stranded on the opposite side of the junction.

The road took a long, slow curve ahead. As soon as he was around the curve, Laird eased back on the accelerator and turned down a narrow sidestreet. He made a quick, tyre-squealing three-point turn under the nose of a startled taxi driver, then braked the Simca to a halt facing out towards the main road.

Seconds ticked past on the softly lit dashboard clock. Then the black-clad motorcyclist went roaring past and Laird quietly set the Simca moving again, following the man, letting the gap between them widen, and gambling on what was going to happen next.

Some time passed before the rider ahead seemed to accept that he'd lost his quarry. But finally he stopped beside a brightly lit pavement telephone booth, left his machine, and entered the booth.

Pulling in a safe distance back, Laird switched off his lights and waited. The rider had to remove his helmet to use the telephone; he had a young face with long, mousey hair.

It was a brief call. The man returned to his machine, fastened his helmet again, and rode off at a slower pace.

Laird followed. Streets and shops flowed past, the motorcyclist skirted the old Rosenburg Castle, and Copenhagen's centre loomed ahead. Heavier traffic forced Laird to reduce the gap as they neared the S.A.S. airline terminal—and he was glad he had, when the rider made an unexpected right turn into a small street.

It was a street where, despite the hour, every shop was open and busy with the pavements crowded and neon signs sputtering. The rider coasted his motorcycle to a halt halfway down, propped the machine outside a brightly lit doorway, and went straight in.

Laird pulled in behind a row of parked cars farther back. He stopped the engine, switched off the lights, looked around, and the combination of shop fronts and the tourist traffic on the pavements was enough. He was in one of Copenhagen's porn streets, where sex, from "blue" home movies to the trivia of pornography, was what kept the cash registers going.

A squad of small, camera-hung Asiatic tourists went past, chattering incredulously. A middle-aged couple in English tweeds, the woman stoney-faced, bulldozed through them, heading for safer territory. Airline bags from a score of countries bumped and jostled as the owners wandered around, some making purchases and the rest stocking up on travellers' tales for the folks back home.

Laird left the car, crossed the street to the opposite pavement, and ambled along at a casual pace with his eyes on the doorway the black-clad rider had entered. A girl blocked his path, raising an inviting eyebrow, and barely shrugged when he shook his head.

The neon sign above the doorway that interested him flashed the invitation LIVE SHOW—NOW. Just inside, where he hadn't been able to see them before, two tall, thin young men with drugstore tans and suede-leather white hunter suits and bush hats lounged against posters which shouted the strip club's attractions in several languages.

There was other competition all around, bars and clubs where even the free-wheeling Danish official attitude was stretched to the limit in four shows nightly style. From the music and noise coming from their doors, business was reasonable though it was still early—and white hunter outfits seemed to be the fashion of the moment for the touts who beckoned and grinned an invitation towards every ticket window.

Laird eased his way back through the tourists, climbed into the car again, and smoked a cigarette while he waited behind the wheel and the passports went by. Then, at last, there was movement that mattered at the Live Show doorway.

First the two bush-hatted door minders wandered out, clearing a path. Then a bald, burly, leathery-skinned man in a grey shirt, grey bow tie and matching slacks appeared, with the motorcyclist at his elbow. The bald man said something to the motorcyclist, who nodded respectfully and took the envelope he was handed. Tucking it away, he pulled on his helmet again and climbed on his machine while the bald man went back into the club.

As the motorcycle came to life Laird started the Simca. He set it moving as soon as the rider pulled away, then kept him on as long a lead as possible.

This time the rider was travelling west, heading out of the city. They left the business and shopping sectors behind, then the rider swung off to the left into a quiet, tree-lined avenue of elegant terrace houses.

Laird followed cautiously. On ahead, the motorcycle's brake light winked on and off while the rider went along at a crawl as if checking house numbers. Taking a chance,

Laird pulled in to the kerb and switched off engine and lights again.

The rider stopped, left his machine, and went over to a house door. He stooped at the door, there was a brief glint of something white in his hand under the streetlights, then the man hurried back to the motorcycle. Starting it, the rider made an unexpected U-turn and Laird had to crouch low behind the Simca's wheel as the motorcycle swept past in a snarl of exhaust.

In another moment the machine had swung out onto the main road and was gone, heading back in the direction of the city.

Laird let him go. Leaving the car, he walked along to the house, which was in darkness. He saw a brass letterbox set low in the door, then read the nameplate higher up: PRO-FESSOR HARALD VASSEN.

He was still staring in disbelief at the metal lettering when short, quick footsteps came towards him along the pavement. The footsteps stopped, Laird glanced around, and he gave a sigh as he saw who it was.

"*God aften* again, Sergeant Kristensen," he said wearily. "How the hell did you get here?"

The tall, angular blonde stepped out of the shadow thrown by the nearest of the trees and came over, her hands deep in the pockets of her denim jacket.

"It was Niels Lundgard's idea," she said calmly. "He wanted to know if you were really being followed. It was— *ja,* 'unusual' is the word." Her blue eyes glanced past him, at the house door. "Like it is now. Do you know who lives here?"

"I can read," said Laird grimly. "Were you on my tail back at the strip club?"

Sergeant Nina Kristensen nodded and her face shaped a frown.

"That was interesting too, Mr. Laird," she said slowly. "You see, I was attached to the city vice squad before I was transferred to the harbour division—"

"It must have been a quiet life," said Laird sardonically. "What did you do? Pull in the occasional litter lout?"

"Not always. Our law tolerates in small ways, but it ends there." She shrugged absently, still puzzled and showing it. "Your motorcyclist met an Englishman who calls himself Peter Hamilton. The 'Live Show' club is owned by Hamilton but he has other interests we'd like to know more about."

"How about his messenger boy?"

"Local help, the kind you buy in bulk." Sergeant Kristensen paused, almost reluctant to go on. "What I can't understand is that he came here—"

"With a message for Vassen," finished Laird stonily. "Is that going to make Niels Lundgard feel happy?"

"*Nej.*" She shook her head slowly. "But I don't think we should tell Niels—not yet. Not till we know a little more."

"We?" Laird raised an eyebrow.

She looked around with a calculated whimsy. "I don't see anyone else here. You and I—is that plain enough?"

"All right," he agreed flatly. "But I don't want you following me around."

"I have better things to do, Mr. Laird," she told him flatly.

Turning, she walked away. A small M.G. sports car was parked farther down the avenue and she got into it. The little open car pulled away a moment later with a crackle of exhaust and Sergeant Kristensen gave a brief wave as she drove past.

That left Laird with nothing to do but swear, scowl at the door and its nameplate, then drive his rented Simca back to the Edelstenen and call it a night.

A grey drizzle of rain was falling on Copenhagen the next morning, and Laird, wakened by a call he'd booked with the hotel switchboard, rose reluctantly. The time was six-thirty and it hadn't been a peaceful night. The traffic noise outside the Edelstenen had growled on until three o'clock, dawn had come up on the skyline about half an hour later, and the first trucks of the new day had begun rumbling soon after that.

Shaved and dressed, still yawning, he stuffed the draught of his London report into one pocket and decided breakfast could wait. A few minutes later he was driving the rented Simca north, on his way towards Tostig, his date with the Berserkers rowing club, their Viking longboat— and, more important, Professor Harald Vassen.

It was an easy drive. For a spell the route was along an eight-lane motorway signposted for Helsingor and the ferry crossing to Sweden. When he left the motorway, starting on a minor road, he was immediately in open country. The land was low and green, heavily wooded, and studded with small villages where the cottages had picturebook thatched roofs and shopkeepers, getting ready to open for the day, were scrubbing the pavements outside their doorways.

Passing through one village, he blinked at the sight of a chimney sweep dressed in black, complete with top hat; the man was wobbling along on a bicycle with his chimney brushes over one shoulder.

As a drive, it was like sliding gently back through time —and when Tostig village and the sea appeared ahead the illusion became dramatically complete.

The grey drizzle was lifting. Off the shore, foaming through the gentle swell, a ship with a high, dragon-headed prow patrolled like a ghost from the past. Her single sail was furled on the tall mast and she was propelled along by the bank of heavy oars which rose and fell in perfect unison from each shield-studded gunwhale.

Pulling in, Laird watched the Viking longship sweep by. He could hear the creak and splash of her oars across the water and the steady drumbeat from her stern, which set the rowers' pace. Fascination blended with a shiver at the reincarnated raider—it was all too easy to imagine a pack of these dragon hulls sweeping out of the mist when the world was young, a prelude to slaughter and pillage.

But these oarsmen were different. As the longship passed, he saw they wore sweatshirts and were cleanshaven. One had a tasselled cap, others wore spectacles. Most of them probably had a briefcase waiting ashore. Though a briefcase, he knew, was often the sign of the twentieth-century raider.

The longship vanished around a low headland and he set the car moving again. Tostig was a couple of minutes down the road, a tiny, old-fashioned fishing village at the mouth of an inlet. The car park beside the village pier was almost full but Laird found a space, parked the Simca, then walked out along the pier.

There was a small wooden hut near the end. As Laird reached it, a small, almost elfinlike figure appeared at the hut's open doorway. The man was about sixty, with a wrinkled, suntanned face and a shock of grey hair. He wore an almost equally wrinkled pullover, a sports jacket that had been patched with leather at the cuffs and elbows, and slacks which retained only the memory of a crease.

"*God morgen.*" The man removed an unlit pipe from his mouth and greeted Laird with a polite smile which showed strong, white teeth. "Niels told me you would be along, Mr. Laird—I'm Harald Vassen."

The precise, heavily accented voice had been enough on its own. Laird shook hands with Vassen and felt a mild amusement at the way his thoughts of a possible bearded Scandinavian folk figure had been demolished. Harald Vassen might be one of the greatest living authorities on the Viking age, but his appearance hardly matched.

"It looks like I'm late," he apologised, easing into the shelter of the doorway and using a handkerchief to wipe some of the rain from his face. "Or did they start early?"

"Just promptly—as always." The unlit pipe became a pointer, stabbing out towards the sea. "You saw them?"

Laird nodded.

"Ah." Vassen's small body swelled with pleasure. "So, how do you like our dragon ship?"

"If I hadn't known she'd be there, she'd have scared the hell out of me," said Laird cheerfully.

"*Ja.*" The wizened, elfin face shaped a wrinkled smile. "With oar and sail and sword our Viking forebearers ruled the sea." Enthusiasm kindled in Vassen's voice. "They found America—though that was perhaps unfortunate. They raided and traded across Europe, around Africa, and into Asia. Did you know they fought a war with the Turks?"

Laird shook his head. Harald Vassen hardly noticed and barely paused to draw breath.

"It happened—just as they sold slaves in Bagdad and reached Samarkand. We even know that another Viking force, the Rus, gave its name to Russia!" A gull flew overhead, squawking loudly. The sound halted Vassen and his mood changed to a penitent sigh. "I'm sorry. As any student will tell you, once I start I forget to stop."

"I'm interested." Laird propped himself against the doorway. "Is the ship they've got out the same as the one you loaded on the *Velella?*"

"Almost a twin." Vassen nodded, frowning. "Perhaps

not so fine in finish. We built three—but the third was con-
structed the traditional way, for display only. The others
were more—"

"Commercial?"

"*Ja.*" Vassen eyed Laird carefully. "Does that make
any difference to our claim?"

"None." The longship was in sight again, making a
fast, curving turn. Laird watched her and asked, "Can you
really get this one out to Boston in time?"

"The arrangements are made. She will be on another
cargo ship that sails in a few days—loaded the same way,
crated in sections." Vassen paused and sniffed his contempt.
"Once, she could have sailed across on her own. But now
there are rules, regulations, fool officials, insurance difficulties—"

"The old Vikings had it easy," sympathised Laird. Out
across the water, the longship had completed another turn
and was heading firmly towards the inlet. He wouldn't have
Vassen on his own much longer. "Professor, after you
phoned last night I felt maybe I should have been more
helpful. I—well, I did try your home number later, but there
was no reply."

The lie brought minimal reaction.

"I was out," said Vassen briefly. "A colleague invited
me to dinner."

"Later on, I did think of going around and putting a
note through your door," mused Laird. "But I was too
damned lazy."

"What you told me was enough." Vassen's voice
seemed to chill several degrees. Deliberately, he switched
his attention to the approaching longship. "She's coming in
now—you can see how the oars are beginning to slow."

"Good." The drizzle of rain was almost over. Laird
took a couple of steps away from the doorway, into the

open, then half turned and asked casually, "Ever hear of an Englishman in Copenhagen named Peter Hamilton?"

This time the wizened face momentarily hardened. Then Vassen slowly and deliberately shook his head.

"*Nej* . . . never. Why?"

"You've apparently something in common," said Laird innocently, watching the little man lazily and seeing him tense. "Our local office reckon he had some kind of interest in the *Velella*'s cargo too. Except I haven't traced it yet."

"I can't help," said Vassen briefly, his manner relaxing again. "Come—you want to see my boys bring her in."

The longship arrived at the pier in another couple of minutes. A last few perfectly timed strokes brought her drifting in, the two banks of oars clattered clear with a casual, totally trained discipline, and then she moored. A narrow plankway bridged the gap from her deck to the pier and the first of the oarsmen began streaming ashore.

Seen close up, the longship was about seventy feet long from her high dragon prow to her sternposts. Open-decked except for a small sheltered area aft, her pinewood hull had fifteen oars along each gunwhale—great, heavy sweeps that demanded strength and skill. Nothing was allowed to compromise her design. The rowing benches were bare planking, the sail rigging was primitive cord—even the metal-bossed shields decorating her sides looked genuine enough to be used.

Laughing and talking, more of the crew came along the pier and jostled past Laird as he studied the raider lines of the low, slim hull. Then he heard his name called, turned, and saw Niels Lundgard. The long-faced Dane was grinning—and he had Karen Leslie with him as he came ashore.

"What do you think of our new mascot, Andrew?" asked Lundgard, his hand on the girl's arm. He wore a sweatshirt and jeans like the rest and was carrying an old travel bag. "If you'd made it earlier you could have been out with us too—but I can't say I missed you!"

Karen Leslie laughed. The tiredness and strain Laird had seen before had gone from her face. There was fresh colour in her cheeks, though the combination of seawind and drizzle had tousled and dampened her hair till it clung like a coppery helmet. She wore a lightweight nylon waterproof jacket which hung loose over a sweater and denims.

"How did he talk you into it, Karen?" queried Laird with a mock sympathy. "Use handcuffs?"

"The next best thing. Phoned me late last night and wouldn't take no for an answer." She glanced at Lundgard. "I'm glad I came—but I don't know how the old witch on duty at the hotel felt. A police car at the door at six o'clock this morning looked too much like a raid."

"A patrol-car crew I know gave us a lift out." Lundgard rubbed his long chin, slightly embarrassed. "But I had decided that to leave Karen stuck in an hotel room was no cure for—well, her experiences on the *Velella*." He switched his attention to Laird again. "Did you meet Professor Vassen?"

"We talked." Laird left it at that. As they began to walk along the pier, he gestured to the other oarsmen, already dispersing towards the parked cars. "Are all of this bunch flying out to Boston?"

"All you see and a few reserves—almost forty of us including the professor." Lundgard broke off to answer a shouted goodbye as a car drove off. "We have about seventy members, two complete crews—we put a ceiling on numbers and the club chooses carefully." Wincing, he watched another car shoot away with tyres squealing and horn blaring. *"Jeg ved det . . .* I don't know how carefully for brains but certainly for brawn."

"I got that feeling," mused Karen Leslie. She waited until they'd sidestepped around an old anchor chain, then looked back at the longship. "How much more practice time have you got?"

"Two more days, then we say *farvel* to her till Boston," answered Lundgard, then stopped and swore softly.

The car park was thinning rapidly. But a new arrival was pulling in, Sergeant Kristensen's small M.G. sports car. She slotted it into one of the spaces, climbed out, and headed determinedly towards them.

"Trouble, Niels?" queried Laird as the tall blonde approached.

"With Nina, it's always trouble," said Lundgard sadly. "She's been covering for me—headquarters think I'm working, but I reckoned it wouldn't be the end of the world if I sneaked a couple of hours off from the *Velella* business." He paused and added with a gloomy satisfaction, "The ship is still my case, they say. At least till someone more important can spare some time."

"Good," said Laird, and meant it. "How about that harbour clearance?"

"Granted. The *Velella* should be in the Nordhaven basin by now. But that's the only change—every check we've made has ended negative."

Sergeant Kristensen reached them a moment later. She was wearing her denim outfit again, with the same large leather shoulderbag, and had a spring in her stride which was almost aggressively healthy. Greeting Laird and Karen Leslie with a large-toothed smile, she faced Lundgard.

"Morgen . . . and how are all the little heroes today?" she asked briskly. "Rowing well?"

Lundgard grunted. "Never mind the humour, Nina. What's worrying you?"

"Nothing." She looked deliberately at her wristwatch. "But then I'm not a certain senior sergeant who happens to be wanted at headquarters."

"Now?" Lundgard gave a groan.

She nodded. "And remember, you've been out checking on a possible lead."

"Since when did we have one?" queried Lundgard gloomily. He glanced down at his clothes, then shrugged. "I'll change while you drive—somehow. But—"

"I'll give Karen a lift back," volunteered Laird.

"*Tak.*" Lundgard sighed his thanks but still hesitated. "Maybe I should have a word with Professor Vassen—no, it can wait."

Laird caught Sergeant Kristensen's blue-eyed gaze. She gave an almost imperceptible headshake, the meaning clear. Their bargain remained and she had said nothing.

Lundgard left with her a moment later, heading at a trot for the M.G., and Laird turned to Karen Leslie.

"Had breakfast yet?" he asked.

"No." She sounded hopeful.

"Then we'll start there," he suggested. "After that, I'm going on to the *Velella*. Want to come?"

"Please." She nodded soberly. "I must talk to Sean Peters."

They began walking towards the car park. Harald Vassen was there, standing beside a tan-coloured Volvo station wagon and dwarfed by one of the oarsmen, a big, round-faced youngster with a small, fair moustache. Laird nodded a greeting and Vassen gave a calm acknowledgement, then ignored him and went on talking to the oarsman.

Sergeant Kristensen's little sports car went snarling

away as Laird guided Karen Leslie across to the rented Simca. Laird set the Simca moving a minute later, but drove out of the village at a sedate pace.

He began humming to himself while the car purred on. Karen Leslie eyed him strangely, but he didn't care.

Harald Vassen, world-famed authority, had almost certainly lied to him. It might be very interesting to find out why.

They turned off the main road after about ten kilometres and followed signs that led them to a farmhouse restaurant. It was inland, backed by trees, and on the edge of a lush meadow where fat dairy cattle were grazing. The owner had been enterprising enough to develop out, with a filling station and a tourist caravan park to one side.

Breakfast was a glass of fruitjuice each, then coffee and warm bakery rolls spread with yellow, creamy butter. They ate at a table in front of a big picture window while the early clouds dispersed and the sun broke through in a widening area of blue sky. The other customers around were tourist families from the caravan park and the waitresses were fair-haired local girls in blue-checked aprons.

"Mind if I talk about the *Velella* again?" asked Laird as they finished with another cup of coffee and a cigarette each.

"Why not?" Karen Leslie looked out at the meadow. "It's beginning to seem like a nightmare that didn't happen. Except I know it did."

"Have you remembered anything more?"

"No." Her mouth shaped a slight grimace. "That's getting to be my standard reply—Niels Lundgard asked me the same thing when he phoned last night. So did the news-agency reporter who came around."

Laird had been counting out kroner notes to pay the bill lying beside his plate. He stopped, laid down the money, and frowned.

"Tell me about him."

She shrugged. "He came to the hotel last night, about an hour after you left—he was doing some kind of follow-up story on the *Velella,* and he also asked about you."

Laird raised a surprised eyebrow. "By name?"

"Yes." She flicked some ash from her cigarette, almost amused. "He told me that he knew you were some kind of insurance-company expert from England—then wanted to know how closely you were working with the police and if you had any special theory about what happened. I told him to ask you."

Laird swore inwardly. It was an old trick, effective in its simplicity. People expected newsmen to ask questions and for some strange reason they usually answered them.

"Who was he working for, Karen?"

"Some European news service. He showed me a press pass and—" she frowned, trying to recall, "yes, I think his name was Fredericks."

"What was he like?" asked Laird. "Describe him."

"Medium height, ordinary build, maybe about your age. He had mousey brown hair, I think. Oh, and a gold tooth—it showed when he smiled." She paused and looked puzzled. "Does it matter?"

"I'll tell you once I read his story."

Laird left it at that, watching her for a moment. Karen Leslie had tidied her hair and the resemblance to Maureen was back again. But he was growing used to it, finding it gradually fading in a way that surprised him. Maybe because Maureen had been lazy and easygoing, while this girl, fresh and with the liveliness back in her eyes, was someone else altogether.

Sometimes, when he thought of Maureen, he knew he'd probably been lucky. She might have stayed and married him.

"The police aren't getting very far, are they?" asked Karen suddenly.

"Give them time," he suggested. "They haven't much to go on—yet."

They drew a smile from their waitress as they left. Outside, the air was warming and had a fresh, clean scent. When they reached the car, Laird opened the passenger door for Karen. As she got in, he looked across the yard and tensed.

A tan-coloured Volvo station wagon, identical to the one he'd seen Vassen at earlier, lay partly hidden behind a store hut on the far side of the filling-station area.

"Give me a minute," he said easily. "I'll be back."

Hands in his pockets, he strolled across to the Volvo. It was empty, but a travel bag lying on the rear seat was decorated with the Berserkers' crest of a Viking ship.

There was still no one in sight. He'd had no tail on his journey out to the rowing club's practice session. He and Karen had left the main road to reach the farmhouse restaurant and had taken their time over breakfast.

Yet the Volvo was there, so its driver had to be somewhere near.

Laird began to walk across to the filling station. He was halfway there when the door of the men's room beside it swung open. A figure showed for an instant, then ducked back into the shadows. It was the big, blond oarsman with the small moustache.

Turning, Laird went back to the Volvo, stooped down, and loosened the valve on one of the rear tyres. As the air began hissing out and the tyre started to flatten, he returned to the rented Simca.

"I needed cigarettes," he lied as he got in. "Ready for dockland?"

Karen Leslie nodded, fastened her seatbelt, and he set the car moving.

———————————◆———————————

By the time they arrived in the city and located the *Velella*'s berth at the Nordhaven docks it was ten o'clock. The fire-scarred ship lay in virtual isolation at an otherwise empty quay and a policeman was on duty at the shore end of her gangway. Near her blackened, blistered bow, half a dozen helmeted firemen waited on the quayside beside a large red fire tender which had its blue roof lights blinking. The Danes still weren't taking chances.

They left the Simca and Laird's identification pass got them past the policeman. But they'd also been seen from the ship. As they topped the gangway and stepped aboard there was a shout and Sean Peters came to meet them. Shaved and wearing a clean uniform, the *Velella*'s chief officer looked a lot better than when Laird had seen him last. But his left arm was still in a sling and his red-rimmed eyes remained those of a man hungry for sleep.

"Karen." His harsh Liverpool voice held a softer note. "How are you feeling now, girl?"

"All I needed was sleep." She looked at him deliberately. "The way you do."

"Soon," promised Peters. He shoved his cap back on his head, showing the stubbled line of his wiry red hair, and glanced at Laird. "Thanks for seeing she was all right. Have you heard anything fresh from the police?"

Laird shook his head. Grunting, Peters thumbed towards the bow.

"If you still want to help, Laird, your local man is up there, rubbernecking. Get rid of him, will you? I've had enough." One red-rimmed eye winked at Karen. "Come on, girl—if he wants a drink with us, he'll have to earn it."

Laird found himself left alone on the deck. Sighing, he headed for'ard and saw a bulky figure in a long, grubby raincoat peering down over the lip of number-one hatch, which was still open.

"What the hell are you doing here, Jensen?" he asked curtly.

"Uh? *God morgen,* Andrew," said Per Jensen in a near squeak as he turned around, surprised. An immediate smile creased his fat, unpleasant face. "I was interested. I thought I would see for myself—"

"Meaning you've nothing better to do?" Laird found it hard to be pleasant to the man, even if he did rate as local agent and almost part of the Clanmore family. "You're supposed to be on bonus time, remember?"

"*Ja.*" Jensen's eyes narrowed at the mention of money. He came closer, looked around carefully though they had the whole area of deck to themselves, and lowered his voice. "But I also wanted to talk with you."

"Well?" Laird tried to ignore the man's pungent breath.

"You know Sergeant Lundgard is still in charge of this case?" Jensen's piping voice held a cynical note. "My headquarters contact says that is true—but only to cover the possibility that the fire was an insurance fraud. The real feeling there is that it might be something else, maybe a terrorist-squad operation—"

"With her kind of cargo?" Laird was sceptical and didn't hide it.

"They've had some kind of hint," insisted Jensen. "I can't find out how strong, but they're working on it, even if Lundgard doesn't know." He moistened his flabby lips. "Something else—I had a strange telephone call to my office this morning. It concerned you."

"How?" asked Laird suspiciously.

"It was a man who began with asking how he should make a claim for cargo he had had on the *Velella*"—Jensen grinned cunningly—"except when I checked afterwards it didn't exist. While we were talking, he said he had heard you were here. But then he said he had also heard you were really from the English police, that your insurance capacity was just a cover—"

"Did he give a name?" asked Laird slowly.

"*Ja*. He called himself Fredericks. Well-spoken—and like I said, very interested in you."

Laird swore aloud. "What did you tell him?"

"Nothing." Jensen gave a sly grin. "That way, he can stay worried, eh?"

"Thanks," said Laird sarcastically. "It happens that another Fredericks talked to Karen Leslie and claimed to be a news-agency reporter."

Jensen blinked. "If he is a reporter, I can check on him—I will speak to a couple of people I know."

"Do that. And we'll leave talking about terrorists till they surface." Laird brought the draught report for London from his pocket. "You can get this on its way for me. When that's done, I'm interested in an Englishman named Peter Hamilton—"

"The strip-club man?" Jensen's fat face gave a leer of surprise. "*Ja*, I know him. The only terrorist thing about Hamilton is his prices." He tucked the report sheets away in a pocket, then gave a wink. "I could take you along there tonight. I hear he has some new girls."

"And I know who'd end up paying for it," said Laird bleakly. "Just find out about Hamilton. All you can, including any sidelines he operates and if there's been any gossip about him lately."

Jensen looked disappointed. But he nodded, took a last look down into the hold, gave a tutting headshake, then plodded off towards the gangway. Laird went to the *Velella*'s rail and stayed there until he saw that Jensen was ashore. Then, as the fat man's ludicrously long raincoat vanished from sight around a dock shed, he glanced at his watch and set off for Sean Peters' cabin.

———————

Two minutes later, standing in the cabin, he had the distinct impression that he had arrived at the wrong moment. Sean Peters was perched on the edge of his bunk, a drink clutched in his good hand, an awkwardly embarrassed expression on his rugged face, Karen Leslie seated in a chair across the cabin and frowning at him. Whatever they'd been discussing, the conversation died abruptly as Laird entered.

"I got rid of Jensen for you," said Laird.

"Thanks." Peters grimaced his relief. "That man is a creep."

"But he knows his job," answered Laird wryly. "So we keep him."

Peters nodded gloomily. "Maybe that's how the owners feel about me." He saw Laird's raised eyebrow and nodded. "I haven't told Karen yet, but they cabled this morning. I take over as master on the *Velella* once repairs are complete."

"Congratulations," said Laird.

"I'm glad too, Sean," said Karen Leslie quietly.

"Thanks." He shrugged at her. "I'd be a lot happier if it hadn't happened and your uncle was still around, girl." He finished his drink and set the empty glass down on the bunk. "Laird, I'm going ashore soon for a spell. Karen says she'll come with me and we'll visit the two men I've got in hospital—smuggle them in booze and fags or something. But after that, I could use your advice."

"There's no charge," said Laird easily.

"Can I treat any cargo left in the for'ard holds as an insurance write-off? Bring in a bucket crane and some trucks and dump the lot?"

"Not yet," said Laird cautiously. "I need agreement from London on that—but I've already suggested it."

Peters shrugged. "Then it'll have to wait and I can give a few more of the crew shore leave—they deserve it." His voice thickened angrily. "Every time I think what happened, with Captain Sloan dead—"

"The man who caused that is in the same mortuary," mused Laird.

"Is that supposed to even things?" asked Peters harshly. "Karen's been talking about shipping the Old Man's body home. But we can't even do that till the police agree to the release."

"Niels Lundgard says that shouldn't be too long," soothed Karen.

Laird nodded agreement. "And they're working hard on trying to find out who your Olaf Hansen really was." A thought struck him. "While I'm here, how about letting me see his cabin?"

Peters got to his feet, beckoning them to follow. They went out and he led them along a companionway where two seamen were clearing broken, fire-blackened glass from some deckhouse windows. Going through a bulkhead door,

Peters entered another companionway, then gestured towards the first of a row of cabins.

"This one," he said shortly. "The police are finished with it." Glancing oddly at Karen Leslie, he added, "She had the next one."

The cabin door lay open, still smudged here and there with grey fingerprint powder. Laird went in and looked around the small space which had belonged to the man they still knew only as Hansen.

It was less than half the size of Peters' cabin, and it had all the appearance of having been hit by a tornado. The police who had searched through it had obviously stopped just short of a demolition job.

"Did they find anything?" he asked.

"Nothing that mattered." Peters gave Karen the same old-fashioned look. "Just his own things—nothing else."

She flushed. "You said that before, Sean—just before Andrew arrived. All right, so I'll ask you again. What's it supposed to mean?"

Peters shrugged. "It can keep, girl."

"I want to know now," she countered angrily.

"Well, I think it's nobody's business what you do, girl," said Peters, and gave a reluctant sigh. "Hell, you weren't to guess what was going to happen. But I just didn't like the idea of it being known you were in this murdering swine's cabin."

She stared at him. "Who says I was?"

"Weren't you?" Peters reached into an inside pocket of his uniform jacket and brought his hand out again sadly. "Look, girl, I took a prowl around this cabin before the police arrived—and this is yours, isn't it?"

He opened his hand. She stared down at the small, bright object which glinted in his palm.

"No," she said indignantly. "It isn't."

"But it's a woman's necklet, isn't it?" said Peters wearily. "You were the only damned woman aboard—"

"And it isn't mine, Sean," she said angrily.

Laird shoved between them, looked at what they were arguing over—and felt a sudden wave of sheer disbelief. Sean Peters was holding a Viking ship medallion which was a twin of Lundgard's club badge. Except that on this one the well-worn leather neck thong had been snapped.

"Where exactly did you find it, Sean?" he asked sharply.

"On the carpet, beside the bunk." The *Velella*'s chief officer reddened and cleared his throat apologetically. "Look, Karen, maybe I sort of—"

"You did," she agreed frostily.

Taking the medallion from Peters' hand, Laird ignored them and absently tested the strength of the thong. Now they were back with the Berserkers again—and the Berserkers meant Harald Vassen.

Yet the thong was strong, not the kind of item that would snap easily. A tendril of doubt began to grow in his mind, but he decided it would keep till later.

"Laird." Peters managed an uneasy grin. "That thing doesn't matter much, does it?"

"Ask Niels Lundgard once I've dumped it in his lap," said Laird cryptically. He glanced at Karen. "Haven't you seen one like it before?"

"No, but—" She stopped, her face suddenly paling. "His rowing club? The Viking squad?"

Laird nodded. "You'd better stick to your visit programme with Sean. A certain sergeant is going to feel badly enough about this without having any kind of audience."

A squad of the *Velella*'s seamen were carrying out more temporary repairs to her superstructure when Laird left the ship and went along the quay to his car. The Berserkers Club medallion was in his pocket and his mind was a fresh confusion of thoughts that somehow couldn't relate, or, when they seemed to come together, took fantastic shapes.

He was almost at the Simca before he realised someone was waiting there. A lanky, sallow young man in a laundered, cream-coloured safari jacket and matching slacks leaned against the car and gave a cool nod as Laird approached. He had a pimpled face, a small knife scar on one cheek, and a filmy down on his upper lip appeared an attempt to grow a moustache.

"Laird?" the stranger asked without preliminaries.

Laird nodded.

"*Morgen.*" The pimpled face showed complete disinterest. "My boss wants to talk to you."

"How does he know I want to talk to him?" queried Laird dryly. "What's his name?"

"Hamilton." The man eased off the car and thumbed along the quayside. A grey Mercedes-Benz was waiting there, stopped under the shadow of a dock crane. "Okay?"

Silently, Laird followed him over towards the Mercedes. Radio music was coming from it, but the radio switched off as they arrived, and the bald, burly man he'd seen outside the Live Show club got out from the passenger side.

"Hamilton?" asked Laird unemotionally.

"Yes." Seen close up, Peter Hamilton was about fifty. He had a bull neck, a soft voice, big, powerful hands, and was wearing a grey roll-neck sweater with light blue slacks. "You've been asking around about me, Laird?"

"Maybe." Laird heard a metallic click and glanced

around. His escort was propped against the car's glinting radiator, impassively cleaning his nails with the point of a long flick-knife blade.

"Forget him." Hamilton hitched his thumbs in the waistband of his slacks. "What's this crazy story that I've got some kind of cargo-insurance claim against you?"

"I was being diplomatic," parried Laird.

"Diplomatic?" Hamilton scowled past him towards the *Velella*. "How?"

"The ship fire was sabotage." Smoothly, Laird went into a swift lie. "I quizzed most of the crew, a bunch of them said they'd been along at your club—"

"Sailors often do, or didn't you know?" Hamilton gave a short laugh. "But because a mob of seamen happen to spend their money at the Live Show, it doesn't follow their ship has to blaze up later. It wouldn't be good for business."

"The man who planted the bombs aboard knew his way around," said Laird blandly. "There's the chance he met some of the crew at your place and talked to them."

"I wouldn't know." Hamilton's face hardened for a moment. "But you were asking about me."

"Because I thought of coming to talk to you. I like to have an idea about who I'm going to meet—don't you?"

Hamilton digested that and looked mildly amused. "Well, in the process you scared the hell out of a customer of mine. That's why I'm here. You talked to Harald Vassen—"

"Who said he didn't know you." Laird raised a quizzical eyebrow.

"He does, and he called me."

Laird sighed. "You mean the professor hangs around strip clubs between lectures?"

"No." The bald head gave a brief, negative shake. "His weakness is books—he prefers his erotica fireside-style, like some other academics. But he wouldn't like it shouted around, so we have a private arrangement." Hamilton paused, then added casually, "In fact, he had a small delivery last night."

"But now he's all shook up and embarrassed?" Laird grinned, appreciating the careful way he was being sold the story. "Why send you to make the apologetic noises?"

"That was my idea," said Hamilton grimly. "I wanted to know what was going on—and why you'd asked him."

"I asked a few people. I wasn't selective," said Laird calmly.

"Then maybe I'll get a few more panic calls. I've other customers who'd dive for cover if their names were known." Hamilton glanced at his wristwatch, then raised his voice. "Carl—"

Carl pushed himself off the radiator, nodded, clicked the flick-knife shut, and got in behind the grey car's steering wheel.

"Time I get back to the skin shop," said Hamilton with a shrug, opening the passenger door. "Look in at the club sometime, Laird. You might enjoy the show."

"Any Vikings around it?" queried Laird.

Hamilton's eyes flickered momentarily, then he shook his head.

"We had a girl who did a Viking act once. But she moved out with an Arab oil well."

He got in, closed the door, and the car purred off.

CHAPTER FOUR

Two large, very drunk Polish seamen, both in handcuffs and looking as though they'd been hit by a wall, were keeping the front-office staff busy when Andrew Laird arrived at the harbour police station. One of the policemen on duty recognised him, grinned over the seamen's shoulders, and thumbed for him to go straight through to the detective section.

Niels Lundgard wasn't in, but Sergeant Kristensen was at her desk and another detective, a stranger, was pounding out a report on a typewriter in the background.

"Where is he?" asked Laird, nodding at Lundgard's empty chair.

"At the mortuary, trying to coax a miracle from the pathologist," she said cynically. "Sit down—he's due back any minute."

Laird sat opposite her. For the first time, he realised she used a light, expensive perfume. The leather shoulder-bag beside her on the desk was lying open, and he caught a glimpse of a pistol butt. It looked like a .32 calibre Browning but his view of it was blocked by a gay silk headscarf.

"I've got something for Niels," said Laird grimly. "Something he isn't going to like. But I also met Peter Hamilton on the way here—Hamilton set that part up."

Sergeant Kristensen frowned and built a slow steeple with her fingertips. *"Hvorfor* . . . why?"

"Because he says Professor Vassen tipped him off I was asking questions."

Her blue eyes widened, and the fingertip steeple collapsed. "You believe that?"

"Not the way he told it," said Laird obliquely. "How much does he interest your people?"

"When he came to Copenhagen he was working for an airline. Then"—she shrugged—"about three years ago, he quit the airline and opened his club. At that time, he was believed part of a smuggling ring at the airport."

"And since then?"

"The same. Hamilton's name keeps drifting in and out of different cases, somewhere in the background."

"But never enough proof?" asked Laird bluntly.

Sergeant Kristensen shook her head. *"Nej* . . . and I can't understand what he wants with Professor Vassen. You're talking about one of Denmark's most respected academics—even if he sometimes acts more like a circus showman." She gave a quick grimace. "I still have my contacts from the vice squad. They say Hamilton has been quiet lately, so quiet it is like he was waiting for something to happen."

"Maybe it has."

He stopped there as the door opened behind them and Niels Lundgard came in. Lundgard looked even more long-faced than usual, gave them a gloomy nod, and sat on the edge of the desk beside Laird. The other man in the room chose that moment to pull the report sheet from his typewriter, rose, and ambled out past them.

"Find some *kaffe* for us, will you?" pleaded Lundgard as the man reached the door. The man gave a nod, a sympathetic grin, and went out. Lundgard sighed and turned back to Laird. "Mortuaries are not my favourite places. Everyone in them looks so damn cheerful, Andrew—sometimes even the dead."

"Did you get anything?" queried Sergeant Kristensen.

"Only that our Olaf Hansen had an old fracture of the left leg. It showed up when they took X-rays." Lundgard slapped a hand on the desktop. "So what are we supposed to do? Start checking on everyone in the country who ever broke a leg?"

"You've maybe something else to work on," said Laird slowly.

Lundgard raised a doubting, questioning eyebrow.

"They found this on the *Velella*—in Hansen's cabin." Laird brought the Viking ship medallion from his pocket and quietly laid it on the desk in front of the Dane. "Peters found it—but he thought it belonged to Karen."

Niels Lundgard seemed to spend a speechless age just staring down at the little disc of metal and its broken leather thong. His face might have been carved from stone. At last, he reached out and touched the medallion, while his eyes sought Laird's.

"In Hansen's cabin?" There was sheer disbelief in his voice. He moistened his lips. *"Jeg forstar Dem ikke . . .* I don't understand—"

"I didn't think you would," said Laird woodenly. "Could anyone outside of your rowing club have one of those?"

Silently, Lundgard shook his head.

"There's something else you'd better know." Laird glanced at Sergeant Kristensen and she gave a reluctant nod. "Your Professor Vassen has some strange friends."

He told Lundgard about the motorcyclist and Peter Hamilton, then waited for the explosion. It came angrily, directed at Sergeant Kristensen.

"You knew about this and you stayed quiet?" Lundgard drew a deep breath. "Nina, when I need a damn mother figure to hold my hand I'll tell you. *Hvorfor . . .* exactly what did you think you were playing at?"

She shrugged, no apology in her blue eyes.

"Maybe I wanted to save you some worries," she said calmly. "Till I could find out more, anyway."

"Save me—" Lundgard swallowed hard. Then he gave a long sigh, picked up the medallion, and nursed it in his hand. "All right, that part is *lukket . . .* closed till we have more time. This is what matters now."

He left them, went over to his desk, jerked open a drawer, and came back with some close-typed sheets of paper which were clipped together.

"Our membership list—every member has one. Names, addresses, *telefon* numbers." He pulled the sheets into two equal sections and tossed one lot down in front of Sergeant Kristensen. "We'll cancel anyone I remember from this morning's practice, then start checking on the rest. Understand?"

She nodded meekly.

"Good," he said sarcastically, then turned to Laird. "Hamilton and—and the other matter will have to wait. But you'd better stay here." Reaching into his pocket, he gave Laird a slim booklet. "You can read this—I looked it out for you, a thing they printed when the Vassen exhibition was in London."

Lundgard and Sergeant Kristensen went into a close huddle over the list of Berserkers members, scoring out names, then parted and started work on separate telephones. The first few names set the pattern. Some of the oarsmen could be contacted straight away. Others were out or were at another number. But a name wasn't ticked off until they'd either been contacted or someone could say they'd been seen that day.

It was a slow, grinding piece of routine processing. Before they had reached the halfway mark the other detective returned with three paper cups of coffee, then ambled out again before he could be involved. Laird stayed quiet, thumbing through the pages of the booklet Lundgard had given him.

Only a small section concerned the Berserkers and their Viking longship displays. It told how they'd originally been formed as a club by Harald Vassen. He had gathered together the initial group of ex-students and had raised the money to finance their longships—close-to-authentic reconstructions of the vessels which had once ruled the northern seas. The booklet dryly reminded its readers that one longship fleet had sailed up the Thames and torn down London Bridge with grappling irons because it was in the way.

The rest was devoted to the Vassen Trust Collection. Silver ornaments and finely wrought gold jewellery, iron amulets, swords and axes, runestones, museum-piece lamps —over the years Harald Vassen's life work had been to gather a collection which brought the Scandinavian sagas of the past to life again.

Vassen's wrinkled, elfin face, pipe in mouth, smiled out from one page. Lighting a cigarette, Laird studied the picture while his mind wandered.

Could anything as outwardly top-drawer respectable as the Vassen Trust be involved in what had happened on the *Velella*? Insurance fraud was a white-collar kind of crime, and apparent respectability was no yardstick for innocence. Somewhere, there would be accounts, balance sheets, that could show the financial state of the Vassen Trust's health. But even so— He flicked back a few pages and shook his head. The trust did give a very basic outline of its finances. They looked healthy. They were studded with large donations, often anonymous but some from top-level names.

Sergeant Kristensen was still using her telephone. But he saw that Niels Lundgard had stopped and was staring across at him with a strange expression on his face.

"Something wrong?" asked Laird.

Lundgard waited until Sergeant Kristensen had finished her call, then signalled her to stop. Then he came over to them, with the Identikit impression of Olaf Hansen in his hand.

"I think we've got him," he said simply. "The hair colour is wrong and that's what fooled me. But give him fair hair, change the style, and the rest is a reasonable match. His name is Aksel Pittner and he hasn't been seen for the last three days." He paused and nodded to Sergeant Kristensen. *"Kom* . . . you'd better come along too, Andrew."

Lundgard rode with Sergeant Kristensen in her little M.G., Laird trailing close behind them in the rented Simca. It took about twenty minutes to reach their destination, an apartment block on the south side of the city with a view that looked out towards the sea. Lundgard's warrant card was enough to get the pass key from the resident caretaker and then they took the elevator up to the eighth floor.

"How much do you know about him?" asked Laird as the elevator stopped and they got out.

"Very little." Lundgard swung the key in his fingers and checked the door numbers along the corridor. "He became a club member about three years ago and works as a domestic-appliance salesman. He asked his firm for a couple of days off, and was due back this morning. But he didn't show up."

They found Pittner's door and Lundgard opened it with the key, then led the way in. The apartment amounted to two rooms with a tiny kitchen and bathroom, and Sergeant Kristensen picked up some mail lying behind the door as she closed it.

Lundgard walked around the small, neat living room, glancing in passing at a large stereo tape-player, shrugged, then lifted a framed photograph from a table. It was a portrait of a blond, slightly pasty-faced young man in a dinner jacket. He was smiling at the camera and holding a silver cup.

"Pittner?" queried Laird. He hardly needed to ask. Apart from the hair, it was the man in the Identikit picture of Olaf Hansen.

"*Ja.* He won a few dinghy-sailing trophies." Lundgard put down the photograph and looked around. "He's our man. But we've got to make sure."

The bedroom yielded nothing. Aksel Pittner's wardrobe and dressing-table drawers showed he had expensive taste in clothing, but nothing seemed missing. It was the same in the kitchen, where some dirty dishes waiting in the sink and a bottle of milk in the refrigerator made it seem as if the front door might swing open at any moment and the owner come walking in.

Sergeant Kristensen had been checking the bathroom. She joined them again and held out a small, dark bottle.

"Hair dye, Niels," she said quietly. "It was in a cabinet."

"Black?" queried Laird.

She nodded. "Theatrical dye—like a rinse. It would wash straight out again with the right shampoo."

Lundgard looked around the apartment again and swore bitterly. Then they began a real search.

It took an hour. It yielded a Mauser pistol and two clips of ammunition hidden behind the kitchen sink—and nothing else. Nothing, at least, until Lundgard turned his attention to the small bundle of unopened letters that had been behind the door. Some were bills and circulars, one was a Berserkers Club newsletter, then he ripped open the last envelope, which was bulkier than the rest, and gave a grunt of annoyance as an airline ticket fell out and landed on the carpeted floor.

Laird picked up the ticket, saw the booking details, and glanced at Lundgard.

"Did you know he was going to Boston?" he asked quietly.

"Not with the rowing team—he wasn't even a reserve." Puzzled, Lundgard took the ticket, studied it, then chewed his lip. "This flight is a day earlier than the one we're booked on—"

"And the reservation is for Olaf Hansen again," murmured Sergeant Kristensen, reading over his shoulder. "Why?"

Laird shrugged. That was something none of them could answer. All that was sure was that Aksel Pittner wouldn't be going anywhere—except, eventually, when his charred corpse was removed from the police mortuary to its final resting place.

Lundgard gave a sigh and spent a moment scratching his long chin.

"Nina, take that photograph of Pittner to Karen Leslie," he said soberly. "Let's try to make this more positive. I'll stay here and start the usual things moving." Then he hesitated and glanced sideways at Laird. "That leaves the other business of Hamilton and Professor Vassen, I know—"

"Why not leave that over?" suggested Laird softly. "Tell him about Pittner, nothing more." He gave Lundgard a faint, encouraging grin. "Vassen doesn't have to be involved, Niels. But if he is, he'll keep—and so will Hamilton."

Lundgard wasn't fooled. "Exactly what are you planning to do?"

Laird shrugged innocently. "I might go along and talk to Vassen about an insurance problem. Any objections?"

Undecided, Lundgard chewed his lip again and glanced at Sergeant Kristensen. She gave a small, encouraging nod.

"*Ja*, I suppose so," said Lundgard heavily. "But stay away from Hamilton—he could be dangerous. I mean that."

He looked at the airline ticket in his hands, then suddenly, viciously, threw it down on the table.

It was noon when Andrew Laird got back to the Edelstenen Hotel. As soon as he got to his room he checked with the hotel switchboard but there were no messages waiting for him. Per Jensen might be on the prowl, but the fat, unpleasant local agent needed time like anyone else.

Collecting a can of beer from the refrigerator, Laird took a long swallow from it, then went over to the window and looked out. Down below, the city was baking under the midday sun. The people on the streets were in summer dresses or shirt sleeves and the lake was crammed with little pleasure boats.

He stayed at the window a moment longer, a half-formed idea stirring in his mind. Then, nursing the beer, he went over to the telephone and asked the hotel switchboard for an international call to the Clanmore Alliance office in London.

Direct-dialled, the call took under a minute to come through, and in another moment the thin, querulous voice of Osgood Morris, general manager of the marine-claims department, came on the line.

"Still enjoying yourself out there, I hope?" asked Morris sarcastically. "Your telex report is in—and I'd be grateful if you'd stop playing around with bombs. You're in Copenhagen to work, not to worry our pension department. And if the chairman starts asking me about results—"

"Stuff the chairman," said Laird cheerfully. "Don't tell me you haven't seen him yet?"

"Not this morning—ah—he's at a board meeting." Morris cleared his throat quickly. "But no doubt later—"

"No doubt," agreed Laird dryly. Morris trotted in and out of the chairman's office like a personal office boy, and nursed hopes of a directorship someday. If that ever happened, he had earned it in shoe leather. "Osgood, the *Velella* job is getting complicated."

"You mean expensive," complained Morris in a crackle over the line. "That damned local man, Jensen—"

"Is earning his corn—I hope." Laird stopped him before he could get going. "Osgood, are you still friendly with that boss cop at Scotland Yard—the one who squares your parking tickets?"

"I—uh—have certain connections, yes." Morris was stuffily cautious. "Why? What have you done this time?"

"Nothing, but somebody here has the notion I'm working for the English police and is worried about it." Laird paused and decided that was enough of an explanation. "Can you find out if they've any case on their books with a possible Danish connection?"

"Yes, easily enough." Morris sounded relieved. "That's all?"

"For now," agreed Laird. "But it could be important, so the quicker the better. Call me at the hotel, or leave a message with Jensen—but no one else."

Morris gave a final mutter and hung up. Laird replaced his own receiver, waited a moment, then lifted it again, dialled the Hotel Brochen's number, and asked hopefully for Karen Leslie. But he was out of luck; she still hadn't returned.

He ate lunch alone, at a little restaurant a few doors along from the Edelstenen. Avoiding the house specialty, curried eel, he settled for steak followed by a dessert which seemed ninety per cent thick whipped cream. After that, deciding he might not feel like eating for another month, he used the restaurant's pay telephone to call Harald Vassen's home number.

Vassen was in, but his voice froze a little when he heard who was calling.

"Niels Lundgard has been in touch already, Mr. Laird," began Vassen. "I know about Pittner, though it is a shock—"

"It also raises complications about your claim," said Laird flatly. "That's what I want to talk about. Not the Hamilton business, in case you're wondering—he explained that to me."

"*Ja* . . . I admit I was foolish. In fact, I apologise." Vassen paused, then gave a sigh. "Very well, come over now if you wish."

Ten minutes later Andrew Laird parked the rented Simca under the shade of a plane tree near Harald Vassen's home. Fallen leaves stirred beneath his feet as he got out and walked along the quiet avenue of mellowed brick terrace houses, each with their steep tiled roofs and ivy greenery, and the air seemed cooler.

When he reached Vassen's house and rang the bell, the door was opened by a plump, middle-aged housekeeper. He was expected, and she led him along a dark, teak-panelled hallway to the rear of the house. Then, pausing, she knocked on a door, opened it, and smiled an invitation for him to enter.

Laird went in. As the door closed behind him, Harald Vassen rose from behind a desk near a large bow window and greeted his visitor with an unexpected smile.

"*Kom ind* . . . come in, Mr. Laird." Vassen was as shabbily dressed as ever, but his wrinkled face seemed relaxed and confident. He waved Laird into an armchair opposite, then sat down again, his small figure almost disappearing behind the width of the desk. His hand hovered over a bell-push. "Would you like a drink, or some *kaffe?*"

"Another time, not right now," Laird thanked him, looking around.

The garden outside the bow window was a riot of summer flowers. But the room itself was what mattered. It was big, one long wall lined with books from floor to ceiling.

His eyes widened as he saw a massive battle-axe which had pride of place above the door through which he'd just entered. The wooden haft was bound with cracked, disintegrating leather, but even though the bright steel head was pitted with age the blade still looked sharp enough to shave with. Old shields and spearheads shared space with other relics on the opposite wall, all of them framing around a large map of the world which was studded with tiny marker flags.

"All from the Viking age, Mr. Laird—except the map, of course," said Vassen, as if reading his mind. "I use it when researching, to focus my thoughts." He gestured towards the map in a vague, encompassing way. "In the ninth century, for instance, Vikings ravaged through the Mediterranean, reached Italy, put Pisa to the sword, then took slaves in North Africa. North America came a little later—but we know they had a colony in Newfoundland about the year 1000. Eventually, of course, Eskimos or Indians wiped them out."

"There were a lot of them about," agreed Laird solemnly.

Vassen blinked, then nodded. "*Ja* . . . and of course that isn't why you came. You—ah—said there might be new problems about paying our claim. Why?"

"Aksel Pittner—and the fact that he was one of your Viking squad," said Laird bluntly. "I've a claims manager in London who could argue we shouldn't pay out until we know Pittner's exact motives."

Vassen winced. "Do you mean you suspect either the rowing club or the trust?" He gave a dazed smile. "Surely not, Mr. Laird."

"Let's say we're cautious. We don't even necessarily go along with the police reports," warned Laird. "But it would help if we knew more about Pittner. How did he rate in the Berserkers?"

"Not highly." Vassen's hand strayed out towards a disc-shaped paperweight of rough crystal lying on his desk, and he began to worry it with his fingers. "At my age and with my experience, I can judge most men quickly. But I made a mistake with Aksel Pittner—perhaps I even share some responsibility in his death and what he did."

Laird shrugged. "People make mistakes."

The elfin face opposite frowned. "Pittner wanted to join the rowing club, and came to me about it. He had been a student of mine, he had won prizes for sailing—and I put him straight into our first crew. For a time he fitted in well, but then difficulties began."

"Difficulties?"

"Pittner became lazy, he missed practices. He was downgraded to a reserve when our longship crew went to London. Then"—Vassen shrugged—"two weeks ago I dropped him altogether when I chose the crew for Boston. I told him here, in this room, Mr. Laird."

Laird looked around at the collected relics on the wall. A tiny, whimsical corner of his mind wondered if they were insured against theft.

"How did he react?" he asked.

"*Ikke videre godt* . . . very badly. He called me an old fool, which I may be. Then there were a few more insults, and I said the club would be happier without him." Vassen stopped worrying the piece of crystal quartz, laid it down, and pursed his lips. "So perhaps I have some responsibility for what happened."

"Because Pittner left here with a grudge?" Laird sat back and put on a doubtful expression. "Professor, how does a man like Pittner get hold of two custom-built firebombs? You can't buy them at the average corner shop."

"Perhaps he knew someone." Vassen shook his head.

Laird could have laughed but didn't. Harald Vassen's story had come earnestly but so easily that he must have been practising it. As a story, it only fitted where it touched —just like the story he'd heard earlier to explain Peter Hamilton's involvement.

"Professor, did you know we found an airline ticket to Boston at Pittner's apartment?" he asked quietly.

For a moment, something like genuine surprise showed in Harald Vassen's small, bright eyes. Then, slowly, he shook his head again.

"*Nej* . . . I did not." He moistened his lips. "He must have been deranged."

"Or something." Deliberately, Laird got up to go, and immediately, with not-quite-concealed relief, Vassen rose and came around from behind his desk.

"What happens now?" he asked. "To our claim for the longship, I mean. There are people I have to advise, Mr. Laird—"

"London makes the decisions," reminded Laird.

Vassen nodded sadly and left it at that. Then, as he reached the door, he stopped and looked up at the battle-axe above it. "You know, it is very strange."

"What is?" asked Laird, curious.

"The way Pittner was killed by his own attempt at revenge—it was almost retribution." Vassen still considered the glinting blade. "The Vikings of old would have said he 'kissed the thin lips of the axe.' That there was a penalty, and he paid it."

Laird said nothing. If Niels Lundgard hadn't told Vassen what they knew about the firebomb, then it could stay that way. They left the study and walked through the hallway to the main door. Opening it, Vassen gave a wan smile.

"I hope you understand the reason for what happened earlier, about Hamilton—" he began.

"Hamilton?" Laird's expression didn't change. "I'm not interested in dirty books, Professor. Not when you put them beside murder and arson."

Vassen winced, gave a nod, and Laird left. The door closed behind him and a small, tight grin crossed his face as he started back towards the Simca. That one, at least, had got home and had hurt.

The sun was hot on his back and he was glad he'd left the car in the tree's shade. Laird reached it, then stopped with one hand already on the door handle. Three men were coming across the avenue towards him, walking casually, spreading out a little as they approached. The one in the middle was the tall, blond oarsman with the small moustache who had been with the Volvo station wagon earlier. His companions were also fair-haired and shared the same muscular build—and none of them looked friendly.

Straightening, Laird faced them and asked, "Looking for me?"

"*Ja.*" The blond oarsman grinned wolfishly. "You

enjoy a joke, Laird. Like leaving a car with a flat tyre, eh?"

"Only when the driver gets to be annoying." Instinctively, Laird tightened his fists. He nodded at the man's two companions. "Why the bodyguards? Did you feel it wouldn't be safe to come on your own?"

The oarsman's face froze and he took a half step nearer. Out of the corner of his eye Laird saw a curtain twitch at an upstairs window at Vassen's house and knew someone was watching. Then the oarsman sprang in with both fists swinging.

But he was clumsy. Laird avoided one blow, took another on his shoulder, then smashed his own right deep into the man's stomach. It brought a whoop of pain, the oarsman staggered—and the other two joined in.

Laird managed to knee the first in the groin and slammed his companion on the side of the head. He tried to get his back against the car, but the blond oarsman had recovered and was there first. A kick on the leg caught Laird off balance, then all three pounced together and he went down, still struggling.

A face appeared close to his own. He stabbed up at it with opened fingers, heard a scream of pain, and the face disappeared. Then a foot slammed into his stomach and the world became a sudden, retching mist of pain. Another kick took him hard in the ribs and as he tried to struggle up a fresh blow knocked him back again.

Suddenly the blows stopped. He had a dazed impression that a dog was barking somewhere nearby.

"*Farvel* . . . goodbye, Laird," came the oarsman's sardonic voice. "That was a warning. The professor has worries enough without you—so stay away from him. Go back to London."

Laird heard them start running. He was lying almost against the tree, and he pulled himself up, using it for support, in time to see all three men pile into an old Volkswagen. One of them had to be helped aboard. The doors slammed and it drove off at speed.

Gasping for breath, his body aching, Laird clung to the tree. Across the avenue, an elderly couple with a small dog on a leash stood staring at him while the dog barked hysterically. Then, their minds made up, the couple hurried off, dragging the dog along with them.

He looked up at Vassen's house. There was no sign of life at any of the windows. Swearing under his breath, Laird slowly brushed himself down, then limped over to the Simca and got into the driver's seat. He lit a cigarette, drew on it thankfully, then inspected his face in the rear-view mirror and decided he'd been lucky.

There was a red bruise over his left eye and a small trickle of blood was oozing down from a cut in the corner of his mouth. Otherwise, ignoring the aches in his body, he was intact. It had been more a warning than a genuine beating up.

But Harald Vassen had known, might even have arranged it.

Blood from the cut on his lip had smeared its way down the length of the cigarette. Laird opened the car window, flicked the cigarette away distastefully, and sighed. Then he started the car and shakily grated it into gear.

He stopped the car again a few streets away, at a filling station, and used the station's pay telephone to call the Hotel Brochen. This time, Karen Leslie was in.

"Have you seen Lundgard yet?" he asked.

"Yes," she said shortly. "He showed me a photograph and explained. It's the same man—the one who called himself Olaf Hansen."

"I'd like to see you," said Laird. "I mean now, if you can make it."

"Where?" she asked.

Laird thought quickly. "Not at the hotel. Make it the Tivoli Gardens—there's a cafe there, near the open-air theatre. In fifteen minutes?"

She agreed, and he hung up.

———————◆———————

The Tivoli Gardens, located next to the Town Hall and opposite Copenhagen's main railway station, began as an idea a local newspaper editor sold to a king in the mid-nineteenth century. Now it is a twenty-acre pleasure-garden oasis in the heart of the city, with every citizen who matters holding a season ticket.

What begins as a park sprouts exotic buildings from miniature Japanese pagodas to a mock Moorish castle. A score of restaurants is scattered within its walls. A modern concert hall and an open-air theatre are matched by a boating lake and a children's playground, there are dance halls and fairground stalls, a Ferris wheel and a roller coaster . . . and still plenty of room left over for tree-lined walks and floral gardens.

A military band was playing a selection of old Beatles numbers to an audience of tourists as Andrew Laird paid his money at the Gardens entrance gate and walked in. He passed the bandstand, skirted a small army of workmen who were laying out an elaborate fireworks display, and made his way towards the cafe by the open-air theatre.

He was early and Karen Leslie hadn't arrived. That gave him time to go into the men's room, wash away a fresh trickle of blood that had started from his lip, and tidy himself.

When he came back out, the copper-haired girl was just

sitting down at a table. He went over, joined her, and ordered coffee for them both from a passing waitress.

"Well?" She looked at him carefully. "You made it sound important that I come. What's happened?"

"A few things." It was the first time Laird had seen her wearing a dress, a light, sleeveless cotton print with simplicity as its secret; it showed her smooth tanned shoulders and long, slim legs to perfection. "I don't know how much they matter yet."

She frowned, still looking at him. "What happened to your face?"

"Call it a mild difference of opinion." He grinned, and it didn't hurt too much. "Some of Vassen's rowing-club boys don't like me."

"Does Niels Lundgard know?"

"I'll tell him later." He stopped there as the waitress brought their coffee. He paid for it, let the woman go, then spoke again as Karen began adding sugar to her cup. "But what has me wondering is the way that Viking medallion was found in Pittner's cabin."

"Why?" She didn't look up as she stirred her coffee with slow deliberation.

"I'd like to be sure how the neck thong broke."

"Does it matter?" She laid down the spoon.

"It might. If you ask whether Pittner really had that medallion with him or whether there's any chance it was planted in the cabin later, to be found." He paused and waited until she looked up. "Now, if something else happened in that cabin, if he'd been in some kind of a situation with someone—"

She flushed. "That would make a difference?"

Laird nodded. "Leather thongs don't break too easily."

"You're right." She gave a small sigh. "I was in his cabin."

"When?"

"After dinner—but long before the fire, and briefly, believe me." She shrugged at the memory. "He seemed harmless enough, and he'd invited me in for a drink—except that as soon as the door closed he started trying to paw me." Her mouth shaped a faintly bitter smile. "There's a time and a place for everything and I wasn't in the mood."

"So what happened?" asked Laird mildly.

"We had a wrestling match till I half strangled him with his tie and he lost interest. I suppose the thong could have been broken then—where I went to school, we learned to fight dirty."

Laird grinned at her. "I'll remember that."

"So." She sipped her coffee calmly and looked at him over the rim of the cup. "How much does it matter?"

"It means that Pittner's link with the Berserkers Club wasn't deliberately tossed in the ring." Laird paused as a white-shirted policeman, gun at hip, ambled by eating an ice cream. "Somebody used him, Karen. Somebody patted him on the back and sent him on his way, knowing he'd fry the moment he set that bomb—and the same somebody didn't give a damn what happened to anyone else on the *Velella*."

She bit her lip. "You're talking about a maniac."

"No. Just someone with a cold-blooded plan—there's a difference. But maybe things haven't gone quite the way he expected. I think he's starting to make mistakes."

"Then I hope he makes more," she said bitterly. "I went to the hospital with Sean Peters. I talked to those two seamen, saw how they'd been burned—"

"And your uncle is dead." He nodded his understanding. "Just remember one thing, Karen. If any more strangers come around asking you questions, play along with them but tell them nothing—and contact me or Niels Lundgard the moment they've gone."

The cafe began filling up as a party of German tourists arrived. Things grew noisier and it was impossible to talk. They finished their coffee and left, walking around for a spell through the Tivoli's mixture of military-band music, fairground noise, and birdsong.

"Ever heard of a Copenhagen club owner called Hamilton?" asked Laird suddenly.

Puzzled, she shook her head.

"He might be involved. Even Harald Vassen could be in some kind of a tangle among it all." Laird took her arm and stopped her beside a mass of pink rambler roses which were in the peak of their bloom. "I don't think you're likely to matter anymore to the people we want, Karen. But go carefully."

"I will." Impulsively, she kissed him lightly and solemnly on the cheek, then smiled. "Thanks. You know, I still want to know about that other girl."

"As stories go, it's a laugh a line," he said dryly. "Leave it at that."

"No. There'll be another time." She glanced at her watch. "I'll have to go. Niels Lundgard said he might come to see me again, with more questions."

"Knowing Lundgard, I'd bet on it," agreed Laird woodenly.

He left the Gardens with her. The rented Simca was parked nearby and Laird gave her a lift back to the Hotel Brochen. Once he'd dropped her there, he stopped at the first pay telephone he saw and called the Edelstenen.

The reception desk had only one message waiting for him. Per Jensen had called and wanted to see him. He would be at his office throughout the afternoon.

It took Laird only a matter of minutes to drive there.

Clanmore's local agent had his office located in a shabby, low-rent office block in the shadow of the green-roofed Stock Exchange Building, and once there Laird left the car outside and rode a noisy, antiquated elevator up to the sixth floor of the building.

The sixth floor was a rabbit warren of small offices of all kinds. He walked along the corridor till he came to a frosted-glass door which had Jensen's name lettered in one corner, opened the door, and went in. The only desk in the small outer room was empty and the typewriter on it was covered over for the day. He smiled at the sight. Jensen saved money by having a part-time secretary who worked mornings only.

Jensen's room was behind a partition at the rear and the door to it was ajar. Going past the empty desk, Laird pushed the door open.

Then he stopped in his tracks, feeling as if he'd been kicked in the stomach again.

Per Jensen lay on the threadbare carpet in front of him. The fat-faced insurance agent had fallen on his back, one arm outstretched, mouth gaping open as if in mute protest.

And there was a neat bullet hole between his eyes.

CHAPTER FIVE

There was a fly in the room. It buzzed its way over from the sunlit window, circled, then landed beside the pool of congealed blood which had soaked into the carpet from Per Jensen's death wound. The fly took off again as Andrew Laird knelt beside Jensen's body and hovered patiently, as if knowing it had plenty of time.

The single bullet which had killed the flabby insurance agent had been of heavy enough calibre to smash its way through his skull and leave an exit wound on the back of his head almost the size of a man's fist. Tiny fragments of brain tissue and bone had spattered as far as the wall behind Jensen's desk. Turning, Laird glanced at the door.

Heavy calibre and close range—the killer could have fired from the open doorway, catching Jensen still on his way from his desk to see who had arrived in the outer office.

He rose and made a slow, careful tour of the room. Jensen's long, drab raincoat hung on a hook beside the door. The desk was bare of papers, even the scribbling pad by the telephone was unmarked. Everything was tidy. Or almost everything—his gaze fell on a tiny, flattened cigarette stub half ground into the carpet beside the window.

Per Jensen didn't use cigarettes, had always claimed he couldn't afford the habit. Picking up the stub, Laird saw that it was home-rolled and sniffed the crumpled paper with a sudden suspicion. The stale but unmistakable smell of marijuana was still faintly there.

Grimly, he replaced the stub and went through to the typist's desk in the outer office. He used the telephone there to call the police, and, more specifically, to ask them to tell Niels Lundgard. Then he once again went back to Jensen's body and began a quick, systematic check through the man's pockets.

All they yielded was the assorted, everyday junk any man could be expected to carry, including a wallet which held a few hundred-kroner notes and a couple of credit cards. Laird put everything back, tried the raincoat, and found a grubby bag of toffees in one pocket and a set of car keys in the other.

That left the desk. It had two drawers, the bottom one filled with office files and the smaller one on top a jumble of pencils, paperclips, and salvaged string. A folded piece of paper caught his eye and he opened it out of curiosity, then frowned.

It was a sales receipt for eighty kroner, dated that day. The shop address seemed familiar, then he remembered. It was on the same street as the Live Show club.

He put the receipt back, closed the drawer, and returned to the outer office. A moment later, lighting a cigarette, he heard the sound of the elevator gates opening along the corridor, then two uniformed patrolmen burst in. As they saw him they stopped, eyeing him suspiciously, one with his hand on the butt of his holstered pistol.

"In there," said Laird helpfully, thumbing towards Jensen's room. "I made the *telefon* call."

One patrolman stayed with him, the other went straight through. When he came back, he nodded grimly to his companion and used the telephone. Then they both waited, saying nothing, watching him.

More police, plainclothesmen this time, arrived in another few minutes. They ignored Laird at first, then one appeared and showed Laird the marijuana stub nestled in a plastic bag.

"*Vaersgod* . . . is this yours?" he asked with a wooden politeness.

"No." Laird spread his arms in an invitation for them to search him.

"I only asked." The man grinned. "Niels Lundgard says you are okay, an' that is enough."

He was left alone again, reduced to the status of a spectator but with one of the patrolmen posted unobtrusively between him and the door. A police surgeon and a photographer arrived, more men came and went, and another few minutes passed before Niels Lundgard hurried in at last, looking red-faced and flustered.

"You're late," welcomed Laird.

"Go to hell," said Lundgard bleakly, and went straight through.

The photographer's electronic flash gun finished its task and the police surgeon got to work whistling a Strauss waltz. The rest of the hustle of activity went on, then at last Lundgard emerged from the inner office with an older man who spoke to him briefly with an undisguised authority and then left.

"Headquarters brass—they don't like having their afternoon sleep disturbed," said Lundgard wryly when the older man was safely away. He dismissed the patrolman with a jerk of his head, then came over and perched on the typist's desk beside Laird, his long face glum.

"Now, *min ven* . . . your turn. Let's keep it short.

Jensen was working for you, but was there any special reason that brought you here?"

Laird shook his head. "He left a message at the Edelstenen asking me to come, but he didn't say why."

"When did he leave this message?"

Laird shrugged. "I don't know. The hotel might."

"Our medical examiner puts time of death at approximately an hour before you called us." Lundgard considered him awkwardly. "Where were you then, Andrew?"

"With Karen Leslie, at the Tivoli Gardens. Before that, I was with Harald Vassen." Laird touched the faint bruise marks on his face and grinned a little. "If you want an additional check, in between times I had a disagreement with some of your Berserkers pals who think I'm annoying Vassen too much. One is a big blond fellow with a moustache—he mostly drives a tan Volvo station wagon."

Lundgard frowned. "I know him. His name is Bermann but we call him The Ape—he has a wealthy father, and big muscles but little brain. What happened?"

"Ask him," suggested Laird woodenly. "Or Vassen—I've a feeling he saw it too." Then he looked around. "Where's Sergeant Kristensen? I thought she'd have been in on this."

"She's coming." Lundgard glanced at his wristwatch. "I had her finding out what she could about Aksel Pittner."

"Any luck?"

"*Nej* . . . not yet." Lundgard paused and went over to say goodbye to the police doctor, who was leaving. Another detective spoke to him briefly, then he returned. "Andrew, the way things stand, nobody in the offices on this floor heard a shot, saw anything, or knows anything."

"Which means a silencer, with few preliminaries," mused Laird.

"And a large-calibre handgun," said Lundgard grimly.

"Do you know where we found the bullet? We dug it out of the wall behind Jensen's desk—flattened, useless as evidence." His manner changed and became almost a plea. "I need a start point, Andrew, a motive. What was Jensen working on?"

"I'll tell you, but you won't like it." Laird braced himself for the Dane's reaction. "He was running a check for me on Peter Hamilton—"

"Hamilton?" Lundgard stiffened, his eyes suddenly bright with anger. "I told you that was *forbudt* . . . that you were to stay away from Hamilton."

"I know." Laird got up and took the few steps over to the door of Jensen's office. He looked down at Jensen's body, then turned and met Lundgard's wrathful expression. "But Jensen had contacts—the kind that maybe don't talk to a police badge, Niels. All he was doing was picking up gossip."

"He picked up a bullet through the skull instead," snarled Lundgard. "Even if Hamilton did have anything to do with it, he will have a guaranteed armour-plated alibi. And in exchange for a dead man, what have we got?"

Laird shook his head. "Nothing—and don't rub it in. I didn't particularly like Jensen, but that doesn't help, believe me."

Lips pursed, Lundgard said nothing for a moment and gradually a little of the anger left his manner. He beckoned Laird back into the outer office, slumped down in a chair, and shook his head.

"Did Jensen give you any hint about what he planned?" he asked.

"No. But he was near Hamilton's strip club sometime today," Laird told him. "You'll find a jeweller's sales slip in his desk drawer that proves it."

"Thank you," said Lundgard sarcastically. "Anything else?"

"A man who calls himself Fredericks." Laird sketched what he meant, but Lundgard looked unimpressed.

The telephone rang on the typist's desk and, as there was no one else near it, Lundgard answered. Then he turned to Laird again.

"For you. A call from London."

Laird took the receiver from him. It was Osgood Morris; Clanmore's marine-claims manager was in a huffy mood.

"Was that Jensen?" he demanded. "You can tell him I don't like his telephone manner."

"No, it wasn't Jensen," said Laird carefully, glancing at Lundgard, who was waiting with undisguised curiosity. "I'll explain later, Osgood."

"Something wrong?" Morris' voice sharpened. Whatever else he lacked, he had a long-distance nose for trouble.

"Later," said Laird firmly. "Did your friend help us?"

"Yes, but negative. There are no current British police inquiries with Danish links. Or the other way around." Morris didn't give up. "Now look, what's going on?"

"I'll call you back." Laird hung up firmly before Morris could protest. He told Lundgard, "*Velella* insurance business. Just an idea I had, but it didn't work out."

Lundgard gave a sardonic grunt but left it at that as the office door swung open again and Sergeant Kristensen arrived.

He led her through to Jensen's office and they stayed there some minutes while the other police came and went on various errands. Then, at last, they returned and came over to Laird.

"Nina has the story," said Lundgard grimly. "I'm going to talk to Hamilton now—'routine inquiry' will be the phrase. But something else has to be done. Do you know Jensen's wife?"

"No," said Laird resignedly. "But he was our man. I'll tell her."

Lundgard nodded almost sympathetically. "Nina has the address and will go with you. There's just a chance the woman knows something."

They drove out together in Laird's car and Sergeant Kristensen, nursing her inevitable shoulderbag, maintained a diplomatic silence except when she had to give directions. The journey took about twenty minutes. Per Jensen's home was a modest bungalow with an untidy garden in a slightly faded suburb on the south side of the city. His wife, Elsa, was fat and middle-aged and came to the door wearing an apron over her pastel green dress.

"*Fru* Jensen, I'm sorry," began Laird awkwardly. "We have some bad news for you, news about your husband."

"*Taler de Englesk?*" asked Sergeant Kristensen softly.

The woman nodded, staring at Laird. When he told her that Jensen was dead, the fat face went white and seemed to crumple. But she didn't start to cry until they were inside.

Feeling helpless, Laird thankfully let Sergeant Kristensen take over. She made Elsa Jensen sit down in the living room, sent Laird into the kitchen to make some coffee, and talked quietly, calming the woman, until he returned with three cups on a tin-lid tray. Then, as Elsa Jensen nursed her cup in trembling hands, Laird looked around. The furniture was plain and old-fashioned but spotlessly clean and a couple of delicate water-colour paintings hung on one wall.

It wasn't what he had expected. He wondered how much of it, if anything, was Per Jensen.

"She says her husband was home for lunch," said Sergeant Kristensen quietly.

"Today?"

"*Ja.* He always came home to eat—it saved money."
Sergeant Kristensen kept any opinion out of her voice, and
glanced at the woman. "I think we could maybe talk a little
more to her now. I've told her what happened."

Elsa Jensen nodded. Her eyes were still red from cry-
ing but when she spoke her voice was reasonably steady.

"You saw Per—afterwards?" she asked Laird.

He nodded. "He must have died instantly, *Fru* Jensen."

"Per spoke of you." She bit her lip. "He liked you."

Laird winced and asked, "Did he tell you what he'd
been doing this morning?"

"*Nej.*" She shook her head, "He never talked to me
about work. I—" An attempt at a smile quivered on her
face. "He said I would never understand."

"Did he even say where he had been?" tried Laird.

She shook her head again. "But he was pleased. He
brought me a present. Over there—"

Sergeant Kristensen went across to the table she indicated and came back with a small cardboard box. Elsa
Jensen laid down the coffee cup, opened the box, and
showed Laird a pair of cheap ceramic earrings which were
as gaudy as they were hideous. The name on the box lid
matched the receipt he'd found in Jensen's desk.

"They're nice," said Sergeant Kristensen with a determined effort. "Did your husband often bring you presents,
Fru Jensen?"

"He didn't have much money to spare." She looked
away from them, her eyes moistening and her voice starting
to break. "But he told me he had just earned a big bonus
from the English insurance companies and this would be
my share—"

"Think," urged Laird softly. "Didn't he give you some
hint about the reason he was going to get this bonus?"

"He always said I wouldn't understand business," she answered wearily, then paused, her fat face creasing in a frown of concentration. "There was just the one thing he said several times, as we ate lunch—and it wouldn't help."

"Tell us anyway, *Fru* Jensen," suggested Sergeant Kristensen hopefully.

The woman shrugged. "It was that he had always liked spring and autumn best of the seasons—that if he was right, we could maybe even go a holiday in the autumn." Her lips quivered. "He laughed about it, made a joke about it—"

Laird glanced at Sergeant Kristensen and she nodded. They got up to leave.

"We can see ourselves out, *Fru* Jensen," said Laird. "If you need any kind of help, I'll make sure you get it. Someone else from the police may want to talk to you, but that can wait."

"Till I get used to being a widow?" Elsa Jensen said it without bitterness. "*Tak* . . . at least I know one thing. Per had his life well insured. He believed in insurance."

There was no answer to that one, and they left.

———————

Laird set the Simca moving for the drive back to town, conscious that for once Sergeant Nina Kristensen was both irritated and puzzled.

"What's wrong?" he asked, with a sideways glance at her high-boned face. "I know we didn't get much, but—"

"How much did Jensen earn?" she demanded curtly.

He shrugged, accelerating to overtake a truck just ahead, then tucking back into the traffic stream.

"A lot more than I do, Sergeant." He grinned wryly. "A hell of a lot more—even if he didn't look it. That marine

agency of his was a dripping roast as far as commission
earnings go."

She swore with a surprising vehemence, her blue eyes
angry. "Then his wife didn't know it, did she? Those damn
ghastly earrings—"

"That was Jensen," mused Laird. "I'll bet he planned
to put them through expenses."

The road verge widened into parking space ahead and
on an impulse he pulled in and stopped, leaving the gear
change in neutral and the engine murmuring.

"Call it a profound thought if you like, Sergeant," he
said viciously. "But Jensen had got hold of something that
mattered. Otherwise, why kill him? And we know he was
near Hamilton's strip club—"

"Which Niels says is *forbudt,* off limits as far as you
are concerned," she reminded firmly. Reaching deep into
the shoulderbag, she brought out cigarettes and a lighter,
gave him one, took another for herself, and they shared a
light. She drew on the smoke, then asked, "Can you make
any sense of the way Jensen talked to his wife about spring
and autumn?"

"No." Laird paused as a heavy truck thundered past
on the road, the roar and slipstream rocking the little
Simca. "Look, I'm warned off Hamilton. But I've still a job
of my own to do. How about Aksel Pittner? Niels said you
were working on that angle."

"*Ja.*" She half turned in the seat to face him, clasping
her hands around her knees. "Pittner was our firebomb-man
Hansen—it's positive now. He broke his leg about five years
ago and we have hospital X-rays of the healed bone. They
match the X-rays from the mortuary."

Laird nodded moodily. "What else did you get on
him?"

"Only that he spent money freely—more money than

he earned in his job. He had no close friends, but people who knew him thought he maybe made extra cash gambling." She raised a sardonic eyebrow. "I know—that must be one of the oldest stories in the world."

"How about his politics?"

"Headquarters asked that too. But I don't think politics interested him."

"If it's true, it's the first reasonably human thing about him," said Laird viciously. He scowled at the facia clock. "Well, if that's Pittner to date, I'll tell you something about Per Jensen. He was the kind who kept his contacts and anything else that mattered in a mental notebook—as little as possible on paper. But I've still a notion of my own."

Sergeant Kristensen looked unhappy. "*Hvad* . . . remember Niels—"

"Niels is forgetting I've a job of my own to do, one that can't wait," Laird interrupted brutally. "He wants Hamilton, so I'll give him elbow room. But there's a lot more I need to know about Harald Vassen." His fingers drummed the steering wheel, then he gave her a lopsided grin. "I need a tame expert on the Viking business, someone right outside the Vassen Trust lineup. Any ideas?"

"You just want to talk with someone?" she asked cautiously.

Laird nodded. Sergeant Kristensen drew lightly and thoughtfully on her cigarette, as if making up her mind, then glanced at him, an odd twinkle in her clear blue eyes.

"Then maybe the man you want is Arnold Ramussen. I haven't seen him for a long time, but if you told him I sent you he might help."

"How well did you know him?" asked Laird suspiciously.

She smiled and shook her head. "It was a few years back. But I think he'll remember. Will that do?" Then she glanced at her watch. "He works at the *Vikingehallen*, the State Viking Museum at Roskilde. It will take you about half an hour to drive there and if you're going you'd better leave now—he works ordinary office hours. I can take a taxi back into town, then collect my own car."

"And after that?" queried Laird.

Her slim, strong shoulders gave a fractional shrug. "See Niels, tell him about *Fru* Jensen, then report to headquarters. Then, if Niels hasn't done it, I must see Karen Leslie again. We're releasing Captain Sloan's body, and as next of kin here—"

Laird nodded. There were always formalities, even after death. Official red tape could stretch its length right to the very graveside—and sometimes didn't stop there. Reaching forward, he slotted the rented Simca into gear and set it moving.

"Do me one favour when you see Arnold Ramussen," said Sergeant Kristensen with a slight chuckle. "Tell him I still can't stand garlic."

"Garlic?" Laird blinked.

"Garlic," she agreed mildly, and left it at that.

The road to Roskilde Fjord was broad, straight, and fast, and the traffic on it was reasonably light in mid-afternoon. Laird made good time and left a stretch of motorway at a loop junction. A few minutes later he was following signposts which led him through the little town of Roskilde, then along beside the sparkling blue water of the fjord to a large, impressively architectured modern building which was the *Vikingehallen*.

It was built on the water's edge, the waves lapping against the main concrete columns on the seaward side and the sun glinting on its long expanse of tall glass windows. Laird left his car in the parking lot and entered the main hall of the building as a class of schoolchildren, their tour complete, emerged from a cinema area and charged across in the direction of the museum cafeteria.

He survived the rush, found an attendant, and asked for Arnold Ramussen. The attendant made a telephone call, then led him through a long gallery past the skeleton frameworks of two old Viking longships. They reached an office door and the attendant knocked on it, opened the door, and ushered him in.

It was a modest office, with a window that looked out across the fjord and the furnishings were plain and businesslike. The man who strode over from the window to greet Laird was tall and lean and equally businesslike.

"*God aften,* Mr. Laird," said Arnold Ramussen in a brisk, cheerful voice. He looked in his thirties, had thinning fair hair, and wore a well-tailored sports suit with a white shirt and plain maroon tie. "You told the attendant you needed my opinion about an insurance matter—but I hope that's wrong. I'm an administrator, not any kind of expert."

"Nina Kristensen said you were still the man I should see," said Laird.

"Nina?" Ramussen gave a delighted grin. "*Ja,* I haven't seen her—"

"For a long time," completed Laird. "But she thought you'd remember."

Ramussen nodded and his grin took on a slightly sheepish edge. "Did she send any message?"

"Just that she still can't stand garlic," said Laird dryly. "She said you'd understand."

"It was something we disagreed about—there were other things, of course." Ramussen shook his head sadly, then pulled out a chair beside his desk. "Sit down, Mr. Laird. If Nina wants me to help, I'll certainly try."

Seated, Laird waited until Ramussen was also settled. He discovered himself thinking about Sergeant Kristensen in a way he hadn't before, but put that out of his mind as he saw the museum man's puzzled interest. Taking out his Clanmore identification, he laid it on the desk in front of Ramussen.

"I asked her who could tell me more about the Vassen Trust Collection," he said bluntly, then stretched the truth a little. "It goes out to Boston soon. My company are involved in the insurance cover, and there are problems."

Ramussen's smile faded. "Then maybe Nina was wrong after all. The *Vikingehallen* is not connected with the Vassen Trust or its collection—neither am I."

Laird nodded. "That's why I'm here."

Folding his arms, Ramussen considered him with a frown. "You said problems. What kind of problems?"

"Confidential ones."

Laird waited.

"All right," said Ramussen warily. "I can listen, I suppose. But—well, so we understand each other, how much do you know about the *Vikingehallen* and what we have here?"

"Nothing," admitted Laird.

Ramussen picked up a pen from his desk and toyed with it, still frowning. "This place was built to house the largest single find of genuine Viking ships ever made in Denmark, Mr. Laird—five of them, scuttled across the Roskilde Fjord perhaps a thousand years ago to protect the first Roskilde settlement from seaborne enemies. You perhaps saw a little of the ships as you came in?"

Laird nodded.

"Some of the ships were salvaged in thousands of fragments," said Ramussen slowly. "The result is a jigsaw puzzle, one that will take years to complete. When I see the job our people are quietly doing I admire them—and thank God I'm a civil servant in disguise."

"But it doesn't sound like Harald Vassen style," mused Laird, leaning back in his chair.

"*Nej* . . . and it is not." Ramussen tossed the pen onto his desk. It rolled to a halt against a letter opener. "Vassen is a pirate among his kind. He prefers buying from existing collections to burrowing for new finds, he uses emotional publicity instead of a digging spade—yet even his worst enemies will admit that few men alive know more about the Viking age." He sighed. "Even his damn Vassen Trust Collection is in its own way an expression of his contempt for others."

"How much would you reckon the Vassen Collection is worth?" asked Laird mildly.

Ramussen shrugged. "I know a Swedish-American steel millionaire offered to buy it outright for ten million dollars and that wasn't enough—or so Vassen claims. But who sees the Vassen Collection between exhibitions? Only the mice in the bank strongrooms where it stays stored."

Laird fought down a smile at Ramussen's disgust and managed a slow, sympathetic nod. It was time to steer around to what he really wanted to know.

"How about the financial side of the operation?"

"He has a board of trustees, all highly respectable —and the money flows in." Ramussen grimaced at the thought. "Give a Scandinavian the chance to remember his Viking ancestry and you're halfway home—and Vassen knows it, even though some of his biggest donations come anonymously." He stopped suddenly and frowned. "*Vent* . . . wait a moment. Are you trying to ask me if the trust has money troubles?"

"Not particularly," said Laird blandly. "Why? Have they troubles?"

Ramussen gave a humourless laugh. *"Nej* . . . any state museum would like to have the trust's kind of problems, believe me. I read the papers, I know about their longship being burned in the *Velella* fire, but that's almost an incidental."

"Tell that to my company's claims department," said Laird dryly, picking up his identification pass from the desk and tucking it away. "But thanks for your help. I'm just curious about one thing—how much does Harald Vassen get out of his operation in cash terms?"

"A salary and expenses, nothing more," admitted Ramussen with some reluctance. "What he values most is the prestige. In fact, not long ago he suggested the Vassen Trust Collection might be housed here after he dies—but with a condition. The museum would have to be renamed the Vassen *Vikingehallen*. We turned him down."

Laird chuckled and got to his feet. Ramussen did the same, and came around from behind his desk.

"I still can't quite understand why you came," said Ramussen as they neared the door. "Was there something wrong with the first report your people received? When your colleague was here last month he asked almost the same questions—"

"My colleague?" Laird stopped where he was.

"Ja." Ramussen seemed puzzled at Laird's surprise. "The man called Fredericks who came here. Didn't you know about him?"

"Maybe he was from another company," said Laird neutrally. "What did he look like?"

"All I can remember is he had dark hair." Ramussen paused and frowned. *"Ja,* dark hair—and a gold tooth. He arrived here one day and we talked for a spell." Then he grinned a little. "But he certainly didn't come with an introduction from Nina Kristensen. When you see her, tell her there are some things I don't forget."

Andrew Laird drove back to Copenhagen in a thoughtful mood. What he'd learned about Harald Vassen didn't seem to have done more than flesh out the character of the man that had already come through.

But Ramussen had unwittingly handed him a major surprise—the man who called himself Fredericks was no longer just a vague figure on the fringe of the whole mystery that had begun with the *Velella*. If he had visited the *Vikingehallen* a month ago it meant that other factors had been at work sometime before Aksel Pittner had quarrelled with Vassen.

Project it on from there, add Peter Hamilton in the role of a coldly dangerous factor in the background, and the fact that three men had already died—one by chance, two deliberately murdered—it could still be only a beginning in a situation that still had no clear over-all motive or purpose.

And that, in its own way, angered Laird as much as anything.

It was about five o'clock when he drove up to the harbour police station, parked the Simca outside, and walked in.

The scene in the main office was one stage short of a minor riot. A Panamanian freighter had been raided by a combined team of customs and police, and a lineup of seamen were being processed on a variety of charges from drug smuggling onward, by a perspiring, openly harassed desk sergeant. Laird eased past the noisy confusion and made his way to the detective section, where he found Niels Lundgard alone in the room.

"*Kom ind . . .* I hoped you'd show up, Andrew." The long-faced Dane, who was sitting with his feet propped up on a table, gave him a doleful grin and thumbed towards another chair. "Sit down. Sorry about the way I chewed you out last time."

"I expected it." Laird got the chair and used it saddle-style, leaning his arms on the wooden backrail. He felt puzzled at the lack of activity in the drab, otherwise empty office. "Have you seen Hamilton?"

"*Ja.*" Lundgard made it a cynical grunt. "I could have scripted it in advance. He claims he wouldn't know Jensen from a barrel of apples, and he had an alibi on tap—a long lunch and a business session with his accountant." He brought his feet down from the table and sighed. "Nina told me you didn't do much better with *Fru* Jensen—though by some opinions things like that don't matter now."

"Why?" Laird was baffled. "What's been going on?"

"A statement is being released right now at a special press conference at headquarters," said Lundgard woodenly. "A terrorist group which calls itself the New World Revolution claims responsibility for the *Velella* fire and for shooting Per Jensen."

"Do you believe that?" asked Laird bluntly, unimpressed.

Lundgard shrugged. "I've already been told that terrorist groups are beyond the understanding of a simple sergeant of harbour police."

"Then can a simple sergeant of harbour police tell me how this New World mob surfaced?" demanded Laird.

"A telephone call—to the minister of justice's office this afternoon." Lundgard spread his hands in a frankly helpless gesture. "Our counterterrorist people think they match with a Maoist splinter group that has surfaced under different names a couple of times before. Their communiqué, as they called it, certainly led off with the usual rubbish about striking a blow against foreign capitalists and imperialists."

"And that's why they chose the *Velella?*" Laird stayed incredulous.

"This 'communiqué' said they were after her cargo. That it was a warning to Danish firms who traded with the wrong firms in America." Lundgard chewed his lip. "Meaning, I suppose, any U.S. corporation that has links with what they reckon is the wrong side in the Middle East or other hotspots. Vague, *ja*—maybe it's true, maybe it isn't—but they damn well named Aksel Pittner as the 'heroic volunteer' who placed the firebombs."

"With automatic promotion to grade-one martyrdom," completed Laird sardonically. He snapped finger and thumb together. "So someone made a telephone call—like that. But how much of the rest of it do you really believe?"

Lundgard shook his head uneasily. "I don't know. How much use is logic if you're dealing with crazy men, Andrew? Maybe they wanted Pittner dead. Maybe Per Jensen stumbled on something and got too close to them—or maybe it is all a big fiction. But the main result is that headquarters have taken over."

"Completely?"

"*Ja.* I'm right out of it." Lundgard gave a lopsided grimace. "It's a standing instruction. Any hint of terrorist activity and the specialists move in. As far as they're concerned, I've to sit here on my backside and do nothing more about it unless instructed."

Lundgard stopped and waited, the only sound in the shabby little room an occasional squeak as he shifted in his chair. For Laird, it was a complete and still-unbelievable turnaround. He didn't blame the Danes for their reaction—most police forces would have done the same when political terrorist involvement was suggested. The way Aksel Pittner's name had been used in the "communiqué" meant that the possible existence of the New World group had to be treated seriously.

But it was still all too easy and too convenient. Even the timing made him suspicious—the timing and the slow buildup of circumstances that formed a much more likely alternative.

"Does it make any difference that our wispy friend Fredericks has surfaced again?" he asked at last.

"Where?" Lundgard stirred and was interested. "I checked that out. He may have claimed to be a reporter but no one in the business has ever heard of him."

"This time he called himself an insurance investigator." Laird told him the rest.

"All I can do is pass it on to headquarters," said Lundgard resignedly. "I'm sorry, Andrew, but that's how it is. But I suppose there's one benefit in the situation—you can make a full report to your London office now."

"Just tell them it was nasty terrorists, then catch a plane home?" asked Laird sarcastically. He saw the Dane wince and regretted what he'd said. "You know, if we were a couple of dogs we could go out and have a fight somewhere—then we'd both feel happier."

"Maybe." Lundgard grinned, then brightened a little. "I have a better idea. Tonight you and I, Sergeant Nina, and Karen Leslie will have dinner together and relax for a change." He slapped the table. "Agreed?"

Laird hesitated, then gave in.

"Where and when?"

"Eight o'clock," suggested Lundgard. "At a little restaurant called the Tredive, near the Tivoli Gardens—the food there is the best in town. I'll arrange the rest of it—and to hell with headquarters, this is on my expense account."

He swung his feet back up on the table again and began whistling in a sad off-key.

———————◄►———————

One more surprise was awaiting Andrew Laird when, a little later, he got back to the Edelstenen Hotel. He heard his name called as he entered the lobby, turned, and saw the diminutive, untidy figure of Professor Harald Vassen hurrying towards him.

"Can I talk to you for a moment, Mr. Laird?" asked Vassen with an anxious formality. He glanced around the crowded lobby. "Not here—somewhere privately?"

Laird guided him through to an almost deserted coffee lounge and they sat down, Vassen firmly waving away a waiter who began ambling towards them with his tray.

"What's your problem, Professor?" asked Laird more politely than he felt. "The last time I saw you, I got the distinct impression that I wasn't popular."

"I know—I saw what happened outside." Vassen combed a hand over his rumpled grey hair and looked worried. *"Det gor mig ondt . . .* I have to apologise for that. The young fools didn't understand—"

"Now you surprise me," mused Laird. "Doesn't it come under the heading of what you'd call 'Viking spirit'?"

For an instant, Vassen's small bright eyes froze. Then he forced a smile. "It won't happen again. I have made sure of that, believe me. But—"

"But that's not why you came?" Laird eyed him blandly, then slowly and deliberately lit a cigarette. "What did bring you along, Professor?"

"I want to know why you went to the *Vikingehallen* at

Roskilde this afternoon." Harald Vassen made it a challenge, sitting bolt upright on the edge of his chair. "Why you went there, and what right you had to ask a fool like Ramussen questions about me."

"He called you?" Laird kept an impassive face, but mentally cursed the museum administrator and knew he should have reckoned on some kind of feedback.

"He did." Vassen waited with a strained attempt at genial interest. "Surely you could have got any information from me?"

"Do you make do with one reference source when you're researching a project?" countered Laird calmly. Then he let a thin edge of his real feelings show. "I'm going to tell you where I went before Roskilde. I was talking to a woman whose husband had been murdered because he asked too many questions—or maybe that doesn't rate compared with offending your dignity."

"This man"—Vassen swallowed with an apparent effort—"who was he?"

"Just another insurance hack and not a particularly pleasant one," said Laird grimly. "But he didn't deserve a bullet in the head."

"I didn't know. I thought—" Vassen stopped there and shook his head numbly.

"You thought it was over?" Laird looked at the wrinkled, elfin face and felt a thin tendril of doubt. "Look, Professor, if some of your people have got themselves into a jam, now is the time to get out. You've got Niels Lundgard on your side—tell him, if you won't tell me."

"There is nothing to tell." Suddenly, the old precise authority was back in Harald Vassen's voice. He got to his feet, lips pursed. "I resent the inference, Mr. Laird. You may mean well, but we retain the blood of our ancestors—

and they needed no help from outsiders. Stick to settling your insurance claims."

He swung on his heel and walked out, leaving Laird with the distinct impression that trouble for someone hung over the small, determined figure like a stormcloud. Stubbing his cigarette, Laird walked across to a window that overlooked the front of the hotel. In a moment, Harald Vassen appeared at the entrance, stopped at the kerb, and signalled.

A car purred along from farther up the street, stopped, and Vassen got in. It was the tan-coloured Volvo, with the blond oarsman at the wheel. Then Laird stiffened with interest as a second car, an equally familiar Volkswagen, appeared and took station behind the Volvo.

There were two men aboard. The Volkswagen's headlamps flashed once and he saw Vassen glance around and nod. Both cars pulled away together.

Thoughtfully, Laird turned away from the window. Whatever was on Harald Vassen's mind, he wasn't taking chances—and with someone like Vassen, escort could only equal escalation.

CHAPTER SIX

Evening brought a welcome breath of cool air to the city after the stuffy heat of the day. The streets around the centre of Copenhagen became, if anything, busier in a cheerful mood while the bars did a roaring trade.

Andrew Laird left the Edelstenen, intending to drive to the Tredive Restaurant. But once in the open he decided to walk and enjoyed the change. He wore his lightweight grey suit, which had survived being cleaned, and he had cashed some travellers' cheques. For the next few hours he was going to forget about the *Velella* and all that the ship represented.

The Tredive was a small restaurant close to the Tivoli Gardens with the kind of dull exterior which discouraged tourist trade. But half of Copenhagen seemed to have crowded inside and when a waiter guided him through the close-packed tables to a booth against the far wall he discovered that he was the last of Niels Lundgard's party to arrive.

"Now we can start!" Lundgard, resplendent in an immaculate dark blue suit, a startling yellow shirt, and a tie that was a mixture of both colours, grinned up at him. "Andrew, tonight we drink good Danish *akvavit*—your Scotch whisky is banned."

A bottle and four glasses were on the table and Lundgard began pouring. Laird took the vacant place beside Sergeant Kristensen and smiled a greeting at Karen Leslie, who was sitting opposite her.

"I walked," he explained apologetically. "It took longer than I thought."

Karen chuckled. She wore a long brown skirt and an emerald-green shirt-blouse, there was a brown choke-ribbon at her throat, and her coppery hair shone as if burnished under the restaurant's soft lighting.

"Foot-sore and weary?" she asked.

"Just plain thirsty," he said mildly, watching Lundgard at work with the bottle.

"You know our *akvavit?*" asked Sergeant Kristensen. When he shook his head, her blue eyes twinkled. "It is Danish schnapps flavoured with caraway seeds—Niels insisted on it, but be warned."

Like Karen Leslie's, her outfit was as simple as it was effective—narrow-waisted, flared black velvet trousers with a jacquard patterned blouse. Her blond hair was swept up in a style which seemed to alter her whole personality.

Laird looked at them both. Nina Kristensen had left her police image at home for the night, and he decided he wouldn't want to be the judge in any kind of challenge match between the two.

"To our evening," invited Lundgard, setting down the bottle and lifting his glass. "*Skaal* . . ."

They drank the toast and Laird felt the *akvavit* sting his throat. He winced as Lundgard immediately topped up the glasses again. The liquor seemed the kind that posed an outright peril to strangers—but maybe some people felt the same way about whisky.

"All right, Andrew?" asked Lundgard cheerfully. He

didn't wait for an answer and glanced at the others. "Now, will you trust me to order what to eat?"

They agreed, and he went into a serious huddle over the menu with a waiter. Sergeant Kristensen was translating some of the suggestions for Karen's benefit and Laird sat silent for a moment, sipping his drink.

Unbidden, his mind was recalling the telephone conversation he'd had before he left for the restaurant. Two messages had been waiting for him at the Edelstenen, each saying that Clanmore Alliance had called him from London.

By then it had been too late to contact the Clanmore office, so instead he had called Osgood Morris' home number and had caught the marine-claims-department manager there before he could even pour a drink. Morris had simply wanted to know what was going on, and he had told him.

It was the first time Osgood Morris had heard of Per Jensen's death, and he had made shocked noises over the line—then had got down to worrying about the business implications for Clanmore. That was when Laird had hung up on him, something Morris wasn't likely to forgive.

But he had coped with Osgood Morris before. He smiled wryly at the thought.

"Something wrong?" asked Sergeant Kristensen, catching his expression.

"Nothing that matters," he answered vaguely. He wondered about the perfume she was wearing. It was the kind which had probably set her back a month's pay.

"You're sure?" she persisted.

He nodded, then a flurry of waiters descended on their table and saved him from further explanations.

Between them, Niels Lundgard and the Tredive produced a meal which lived up to the long-faced Dane's promises. It began with a thick gruel soup which also contained fruit juice, raisins, and cream. Then came venison steaks, served with candied potatoes and salad, and the sweet to follow was a massive *lagkage* layercake almost smothered in the inevitable cream.

Laird barely managed to wave away the cheese board when it came around, settled for black coffee like the others, and sat back with a cigarette, wondering how the average Dane managed to stay lean and still eat that way.

"Nu, Andrew—" Lundgard cleared his throat and glanced at his wristwatch. "I—uh—promised Karen that I would show her more of Copenhagen by night. Nina said I could borrow her car." He paused and gave an apologetic grin, his real meaning transparently clear. "Maybe I should have told you earlier—"

"You've had other things on your mind," said Laird dryly. "Nina's car won't hold four?"

Lundgard gave a sad headshake.

"We'll survive." Laird looked at Sergeant Kristensen for agreement and drew a deliberately straight-faced nod. "As long as you pay the bill."

Relieved, Lundgard took care of that detail. Then, after a few more apologetic noises, he escorted Karen Leslie out of the restaurant.

"He told me you knew," said Sergeant Kristensen softly. Then she chuckled. "Damn him, but don't worry. I can get a *taxa* cab home from here."

"There's no rush." There was some wine left in one of the bottles they'd had with the meal and Laird split it between her glass and his own. He nursed his glass for a moment, an idea shaping. "How would you like to go to a strip club?"

Sergeant Nina Kristensen sipped her wine, then gave a slow, deliberate smile.

"One particular strip club?" she asked wisely.

"Peter Hamilton's," agreed Laird. "Unless he has anyone working there who is going to know who you are."

She shook her head. "*Nej . . .* it isn't likely. And just why are we going?"

"Maybe to worry him a little," answered Laird, getting up. "I don't believe in terrorists who make convenient telephone calls. Do you?"

She smiled again and didn't answer, but reached for her handbag. It was small, black velvet like her trousers, and when she opened it there was nothing bigger than a lipstick inside. Looking at Laird, she deliberately closed the bag again.

"Well?" asked Laird.

"I'm off duty. I don't have to believe in anything," she answered calmly. "*Kom . . .* we can walk from here."

Two of the slim young men in the white hunter outfits were on duty as before at the entrance to the Live Show. They murmured a greeting as Laird and Sergeant Kristensen arrived, one escorted them to the pay box, then they were left to go on from there.

The interior of the Live Show club was decorated Regency style. So were the help—the girl with the fixed smile who led them to a table wore a high white wig, a cutaway embroidered doublet which was dangerous when she drew breath, and fishnet tights. A four-man group with electric guitars, all dressed as footmen, played in a corner.

Entrance tickets to the Live Show included the first drink free, and two glasses of cheap champagne materialised as soon as they were seated.

The bar tariff card lying on the table, ready for the next round, had a price list two stages beyond outright piracy. Laird grinned. That was the same everywhere too. He glanced at Sergeant Kristensen and she was watching the floor show with an expression of bored amusement. A large, busty redhead was going through the final stages of a routine with a multicoloured silk scarf. She looked as though she'd have been happier with a woolly vest.

The redhead finished to a scatter of applause and a few whistles, blew a casual kiss, and ambled off while the guitar group bridged the gap to the next act. Laird gave the rest of the big room a leisurely inspection. Business was reasonable, most of the tables were occupied, and the customers varied from the middle-aged expense-account bracket to tourist-traffic couples who were making the free champagne last out.

The air was smoke-filled. His nostrils caught a familiar pungency in it, coming from a nearby table where a group of youngsters were falling about laughing. He glanced at Sergeant Kristensen, gave a slight motion of his head towards the other tables, and raised an eyebrow.

"*Ja.*" She nodded her understanding. "They must have brought it in. Hamilton isn't in the reefer trade—or drugs."

"You're sure?" A man in a cream-coloured dinner jacket had appeared on stage with a hand microphone.

"Positive." She tried the free champagne and wrinkled her nose in disgust. "Hard or soft, it's a tight monopoly. They'd leave him dead in an alley."

Laird mentally erased the drug scene from his short list. The man on the stage was introducing the next act— "Lola from Madrid, soon to leave on a special international tour." The announcement brought a scatter of applause, then a whoop or two as a large, raven-haired girl came on stage to a burst of Spanish music.

"Her passport says Mabel Jones," murmured Sergeant Kristensen in his ear. "From Manchester."

"Don't shatter all my illusions," Laird muttered back.

Then he stopped and swore under his breath. The man with the hand microphone was grinning and clapping to the music as Lola began revealing her preference for black lace underwear and leather boots. Lola or Mabel didn't matter a damn—the man's grin showed a prominent gold tooth. He had dark hair. The rest of the two hazy descriptions he had for the man called Fredericks matched equally well.

"Hello, Laird," came a soft, laconic voice from behind them. He turned and met a cool, calculating nod from Peter Hamilton. The burly club owner's eyes flickered to Sergeant Kristensen briefly and without interest. "Out on the town?"

"Something like that." Laird gave him a casual smile. "Your suggestion, remember?" Then, making it an afterthought, he added, "Nina, meet the man who owns this place."

"*Det glaeder*." She gave Hamilton a bored nod which Laird couldn't have bettered. "Andrew, ask him where he gets this champagne. They should clean the bathtub more often."

Hamilton gave a grunting laugh, rubbed his bull neck, then signalled a waitress. "I can fix that."

"Another time." Laird shook his head. "We were getting ready to leave." He paused, thumbing towards the stage. "Fredericks does a pretty good job for you as linkman."

"Who?" Hamilton's eyes had gone suddenly blank, every muscle of his face seemed frozen, and he waved the waitress away again.

"Fredericks—isn't that his name?" Laird thumbed again to the man on stage, who was clowning now as Lola went into her final bit of business. "I could have sworn I was told—"

"That's Hans Asher. Always has been." Hamilton

rested his broad hands on the table, leaning over them. "Somebody told you wrong, Laird."

Laird shrugged apologetically. "It was a man called Jensen—he was working with me, but he's dead."

"I heard the radio news." Hamilton's voice was unemotional. "I'd say he was unlucky. These terrorist characters go mad-dog when they're upset. Where does it leave you?"

"Not able to tell him he was wrong," answered Laird neutrally. He got up and smiled easily at the older man. "Time we moved on. Nina—"

"*Tak.*" She pushed back her chair. "Andrew, tell your friend his girls may look good, but I've got livelier upholstered chairs at home."

Laird looked at Hamilton, shrugged mildly, and they left him.

They were outside in the street, walking past the brightly lit porn shops, when she began giggling—a sound so out of character that Laird grabbed her arm.

"*Nej* . . . I'm all right," she gasped, laughter still bubbling in her blue eyes. "Did I overdo it back there?"

"Not for what I wanted," Laird admitted with a grin, then switched his mood. "How about my choice for Fredericks?"

Sergeant Kristensen walked a few paces more, stopped, and nodded seriously.

"You shook Hamilton with that, Andrew—like you surprised me. But—"

"But if I'm right he'll have to do something about it," said Laird dryly. "Maybe that's what we need." As long as it didn't bring the possibility of a hole through his head, like

Jensen, he thought. That was part of the risk, and he didn't want to win any medals or end up as a name on a plaque in the Clanmore Alliance waiting room. But Hamilton needed stirring—it was a time when the man's usual instinct would more probably have been to let things cool down. "Any chance of your headquarters people keeping an eye on him?"

She thought about that for a moment. "I can check, but I think they are, already. The terrorist angle has priority but that doesn't mean they've thrown the rest away."

"Good." He felt relieved, despite a basic uncertainty about what should or could happen next. And his throat felt dry. "Where can we get a decent drink? I don't mean Hamilton's brand of champagne."

"The carbonated bathwater?" She made a rude face, then looked around the street. They were clearing the porn-shops area and the coloured lights of the Tivoli Gardens showed ahead. "*Ja,* I know a good little bar in the Gardens. Will that do?"

He liked the idea. They queued at the turnstile gates to get in, then went along the crowded main pathway. A dance band was playing in the shelter of a softly lit shelter styled like a giant metallic clamshell. The usual screams and shouts were coming as fairground cars roared around a roller-coaster ride and a stall attendant tried to sell them candy-floss.

They got past that area, skirted a small ornamental lake which was feathered with floodlit fountains, and reached a quieter sector.

The bar was an open-air cafe with a verandah roof and stools along the counter. Apart from a boy and girl who were holding hands and wouldn't have known if the world had fallen in, they were the only customers. Laird paid for two beers and they drank them slowly, watching a rainbow burst of rockets to the east as a fireworks display got under way.

"You said Hamilton isn't in the drug scene," said Laird at last. "What about the positive side?"

"Still just suspicions, but I can give you some samples." Sergeant Kristensen opened her handbag and checked her lipstick with a tiny mirror. She put the lipstick away, closed the bag, and rested it on her lap. "Two, maybe three bank raids, and almost certainly a jewel robbery across in Sweden—though Hamilton is never in the front line. He is more the planner or afterwards the receiver—the fence."

"But your people can't prove a thing?"

"*Nej* . . . not yet." Her profile was etched like a fine woodcut against the dark sky, then the illusion vanished as another cluster of fireworks flamed in the night. "Can I ask you something?"

"Go ahead," he invited.

"Do you know we're being watched?" Her voice was calmly interested. She might have been talking about the weather.

"Where?" Laird resisted the temptation to look around.

"To your left, under the trees." She gave him a deliberate smile and kept talking. "They've been there the last couple of minutes. I spotted them when I checked my make-up."

"We'd better make sure," murmured Laird. "Finish your drink and we'll move on."

They did, making it all appear leisurely. A few coloured lights marked the next stretch of pathway through the trees and they stopped at an amusement shooting machine. A group of seamen and their girls were just finishing a noisy contest of their own and Laird fed the machine some change, then tried his own luck as the group moved on.

He scored low, grimaced, and turned back to Sergeant Kristensen with a gesture of disgust.

"Well?" he asked softly.

"*Ja.* They're with us," she said calmly. "Two positive— there might be a third, but I'm not sure."

"We can let it happen, or we can run like hell," Laird told her. "Your choice."

She hesitated, then gave a tiny nod. "Let it happen."

Laird drew a deep breath. He didn't like the idea but there wasn't much option. The seamen had vanished, there was no one else in sight—and if these were Hamilton's thugs they were a considerably more dangerous prospect than Harald Vassen's muscular oarsmen.

They left the slot machine and walked on again. There was a bright glow of lights ahead through the trees and Laird could hear music. But the stretch of path they were on was black with shadows and small twigs snapped under their feet.

Then it happened—a quick scurry of other feet and two figures sprang out at them from the nearest patch of shadow. Both came straight for Laird, ignoring Sergeant Kristensen. They had knives, they were young, and they wore "white hunter" leather outfits.

That was all he had time to register. One knife blade swung towards his body. He sidestepped it fast, heard cloth rip, smashed the man's knife arm aside, spun around desperately to meet the second attacker, dove clear as the second knife slashed towards his head, then heard a bubbling scream.

The first man was down on his knees, right arm hanging limp, a new scream forming on his lips. Laird saw the other attacker hesitate, and took his chance. Scooping up a handful of dirt and gravel from the path, he hurled it into the man's face, then catapulted himself forward. The knife swung blindly, a fiery sting raked his side, but an instant later he was grappling with the leather-clad figure.

His opponent was thin but strong. Laird held on to the man's knife wrist, forcing it back, then swore as the attacker tried to bite him. He countered with a flat-handed smash to the mouth, which brought a coughing grunt of pain.

Suddenly a shrill whistle sounded from the trees. Laird's opponent broke loose, ducked as a black-trousered fury came in aiming a judo blow for his neck, then turned and ran. His companion, right arm still hanging uselessly, beat an equal, staggering retreat.

Laird heard a soft *plop,* then a bullet sliced through the leaves of a bush beside him. Diving forward, he grabbed Sergeant Kristensen around the knees and threw her down as a second silencer-muffled shot kicked a fountain of dirt from the path before whining off in a wild ricochet.

They heard voices and hurrying feet. A moment later the seamen they had seen earlier pounded down the path.

"What the hell," roared a voice. "Get him—"

Unceremoniously, Laird was hauled upright. A massive fist poised ready to flatten him, but Sergeant Kristensen grabbed the outraged sailor, explaining fast.

The giant seaman swore apologetically, his companions released Laird, and they milled noisily through the trees and bushes for a couple of minutes. But their girl friends were waiting in the background and the same giant seaman called finish.

"Sorry, pal," he told Laird in a cockney accent. "With what we saw, we thought you were roughin' up the lady. Are you okay now?"

Laird mustered a grin and nodded.

"That's the stuff." The seaman thumped him happily

on the back, nearly knocking him down again. "But look, pal, remember the golden rule, eh? Take a bird down a dark lane if you want, but a mugging is a mugging in any language."

Then, beaming, he strode off to join his friends and they left. Laird looked at Sergeant Kristensen, who was brushing dirt from the sleeves of her blouse.

"You," he said grimly, crooking a finger. "Come here."

She did, her face difficult to read in the darkness.

"What happened to that first character's arm?" he demanded.

"He was too busy to notice me," she shrugged, her manner mild. "I broke it. That seemed the sensible thing to do."

Laird swallowed. "Sergeant, I'm glad you were around."

"*Tak* . . ." She drew a deep breath. "But the third man, the one with the gun—"

"Their backup man," agreed Laird wryly. "They probably reckoned a knifing would have looked better. Did you recognise either of them?"

She shook her head. "I couldn't even give a description. It was too quick—all I can do is report in. Then we can hope they turn up at a hospital for treatment."

"And there's not a grain of proof that Hamilton sent them anyway," finished Laird gloomily.

He reached for his cigarettes, then gave an involuntary wince as a needle of pain in his side reminded him that one of the knife slashes hadn't completely missed. Giving a quick exclamation, Sergeant Kristensen brushed aside his protests and opened his jacket. A dark, wet stain of blood was slowly spreading under the armpit of his shirt.

"You're hurt," she said accusingly.

"Scratched," corrected Laird firmly. "First-aid style, that's all." He grinned. "Believe me, if it was bad I'd be on my back screaming for an ambulance. Clanmore have a good sick-pay scheme."

"But you still need it fixed." She frowned at him. "We can take a *taxa* to my place—it's nearer than your hotel."

"I wouldn't dare argue," said Laird woodenly. "Women who go around breaking arms scare the hell out of me."

They went together back along the path.

Sergeant Nina Kristensen lived in an apartment block a five-minute taxi ride away from the Tivoli Gardens. Her apartment was on the fourth floor, almost opposite the elevator, and once she had unlocked the door she led the way in, switching on the lights.

It was a two-room unit with a small kitchen and bathroom, the furnishings modest and mostly in teak, the one real luxury in sight a spread of thick, snow-white sheepskin rug on the living-room floor. Going into the bathroom, Laird stripped off his jacket and shirt while in the background he heard Sergeant Kristensen using the telephone.

The cut was even less than he'd expected, a shallow three-inch gash above a rib. He filled the washbasin with lukewarm water, washed the wound clean, then opened the bathroom cupboard and frowned at its contents.

"*Holde . . .*" She came in carrying gauze and a roll of sticking plaster. Taking a bottle of iodine from the cupboard, she used it to soak a pad of gauze, then gently swabbed along the length of the cut.

Laird yelped as the iodine stung. Then he took the rest of the gauze from her, shaped a dressing, and taped it in place. While he finished the task, she looked at the tattoo marks on his arms with undisguised curiosity. Quizzically, she ran a finger along the length of the Chinese dragon.

"You were at sea?" she asked.

"For a spell." He reached for his shirt and scowled at the way the blood had stained it. His jacket wasn't much better, with two knife cuts in the cloth and one lapel ripped. His next expense sheet was going to have some unusual entries. Whether Clanmore's cashier would pass them was another matter. "I heard you checking in."

"Headquarters want a full report in the morning." Absently, she took the shirt from him. "I can soak the stain out —it won't take long. Go through and pour yourself a drink."

She had fresh water running into the handbasin and was soaking the bloodstain before he could say anything. Laird went through, found a bottle of whisky and glasses on a side table, checked the whisky's label, gave a murmur of surprise at finding that it was straight malt, and poured himself a stiff measure.

He was sitting on the couch, the drink almost finished, when she came through. She draped the wet shirt over the back of a chair, switched on an electric fire beside it, then poured a drink for herself, added water from a jug, and sat beside him with a satisfied sigh.

"Thanks." Laird raised his drink in a silent toast.

She clinked her glass against his, kicked off her shoes, and sat back with her feet curled up under her. For the first time, he noticed that she had a slight bruise under one eye.

"*Ja*," she agreed sadly, reading his mind. "I wasn't quite smart enough. By tomorrow I will have a black eye— which should please Niels."

Laird grinned. He hoped Lundgard was enjoying his sightseeing with Karen Leslie, because the Dane wasn't going to be happy about the rest of it. He sipped his drink again, spilled a few drops on his bare chest, and rubbed them off with his arm.

"Sergeant," he said solemnly. "You're too far away."

She raised an eyebrow, then smiled and eased closer. He put his arm around her and again she ran a finger along the dragon tattoo, but pensively this time.

"I agree with Niels about one thing," she said slowly. "Stay clear of Hamilton, Andrew. Next time—"

"Next time could be different." His voice was sober. Per Jensen hadn't been so lucky—and in his own case, Hamilton's reaction had been even more than he had expected. He sat for a moment, frowning, then a thin tendril of a notion came into his mind. "Nina, ever play the word game?"

"*Nej.*" She blinked, puzzled.

"Try it. I'll give you a word, you say the first word it brings into your head." He nodded seriously. "See where it takes us. All right?"

She sighed, still puzzled, and waited.

"Red?"

"White—like in the Danish flag," she suggested.

"Just the word," he encouraged. "Right? Sky."

"Sun."

"Horse?"

"Shoe."

"Shoe?"

"Foot." She chuckled, but he kept on.

"Spring?"

"Song."

"Summer?"

"Sea."

"Autumn?"

"Cool."

"Knife?"

"Fork."

"Spring and autumn?"

"Niels—"

"Why Niels?" asked Laird quickly.

"Spring and autumn—that's when Niels has special leave, so he can go abroad with the Berserkers." She stopped, her bright blue eyes widening.

"You're sure?" He brought her around to face him. "Always spring and autumn?"

"*Ja.* The Vassen exhibitions abroad are always in spring and autumn." She moistened her lips. "And Jensen told his wife—"

"Spring and autumn," agreed Laird grimly, his mind grappling with a wild possibility. "Nina, you said your people believe Hamilton regularly operates as a high-class fence. That could be the link. The Berserkers go overseas and when they come back—"

"They need Hamilton?" She stared at him. "*Nej,* that means you're saying Niels—"

"No, he needn't be involved in it," said Laird curtly. "Suppose there's just a small group within the rowing club, a small group and Harald Vassen."

"Doing what?" she demanded.

"I know a way to find out," said Laird softly. "And the man to ask, first thing tomorrow. But suppose I'm right. Then suppose Hamilton and Vassen had a quarrel—"

He sat silent, so much of the rest, from the firing of the *Velella* onward, suddenly able to slot into place neatly and precisely. If he was right—but that depended on London, in the morning.

"We should tell Niels." She stirred reluctantly under his arm. "I could phone him when he gets back—"

"And tell him what?" asked Laird without enthusiasm. "We've got an idea. Maybe we can build on it. But let's find out first."

She frowned over that, but nodded agreement. "So there's nothing we can do until tomorrow?"

Laird crooked a grin. "Sergeant, I didn't say that."

"No," she agreed solemnly. She laid her glass on the rug and stroked the dragon tattoo again. "Karen Leslie told me that she seems to remind you of someone—of another girl."

"From a long time ago."

"*Ja.* Most people have memories." She smiled at him. "Andrew, just one thing. Call me Sergeant once more an'—"

He stopped her there and she didn't protest.

———————————◆———————————

It was 3 A.M. when Laird got back to the Edelstenen Hotel, where only the night porter remained on duty at the reception desk. There were no new messages waiting for him and five minutes after he reached his room he was asleep in bed.

He didn't wake until after eight. It was a dull, cloudy morning with the wind whipping the water in the boating lake across the road, and he yawned his way through a shower and shave. Afterwards, he put a fresh dressing on the knife gash on his chest. The cut was clean, it no longer stung, and he usually healed quickly. Satisfied, he padded back to the bedroom, ordered breakfast from room service, then dressed.

A few flecks of white wool caught his eyes as he put away the clothes he'd worn the previous night. He smiled at the sight, remembering the sheepskin rug at Nina Kristensen's flat. But they also acted as a reminder in a different way. The next few hours should prove whether the almost outrageous theory he'd built around the *Velella* fire had any firm foundation.

Breakfast came. He ate slowly, smoked two cigarettes, then decided the Clanmore office in London would be open for business.

As usual, his telephone call got through quickly. Osgood Morris came on the line, and for once he couldn't blame the marine-claims-department manager for sounding cool.

"All right, I hung up on you last night and I'm sorry," said Laird penitently. "But this time I need your help—it's important."

"Oh?" Morris stayed cool. "I don't feel in a helpful mood."

"If this one works, you're going to have a real report to make to the chairman." Laird let the bait dangle for a moment. "Credit should go where it's due, Osgood—and you're key. I'd be the first to say so."

"From you that's unusual." Morris thawed cautiously. "But go on."

"The Vassen Trust Collection was on exhibition in London in the spring. Their Viking longship sideshow was in London at the same time." Laird nursed the receiver, then went on deliberately. "Osgood, I want to know if there was any major robbery in London while they were over. Major and unsolved. If there was, then work back from there—check every other overseas showing of the Vassen Collection that had the Viking longship along. The same question, going back over the last two or three years."

There was a stunned silence for a moment from the other end of the line. Then he heard a sound like a gulp.

"I'm not going to ask why," declared Morris desperately. "No, I'm not going to ask. But I'll need a couple of hours."

"I'll ring you," said Laird, grinning at the mouthpiece. "Thanks."

He hung up and was trying to coax a final cup of tepid coffee from the breakfast pot when he heard a knock on the room door. Going over, he opened it.

"*God morgen,*" said a distinctly worried-looking Niels Lundgard, leaning against the wall. "Can we have a talk, Andrew?"

Laird thumbed him in, closed the door, and nodded towards the breakfast table.

"I can get some fresh coffee sent up," he offered.

"Coffee, hell." Lundgard rubbed his long chin, scowled, then glanced hopefully at the refrigerator. "But I could use a beer."

"Help yourself." Laird watched as the Dane took a can and jerked the ring-tab free. Then, as Lundgard took a swallow and went over to the window, he asked mildly. "How did the sightseeing work out last night?"

"Karen liked it. We had a good time." Lundgard sighed and stayed where he was, looking down at the traffic below. "Everything was good—then I got to my desk this morning and read a copy of Nina's report."

"About last night?" Laird waited, certain of one thing. For once, Sergeant Nina Kristensen certainly wouldn't have lodged a full report.

"*Ja,* last night." Lundgard swung around from the window, his beer slopping unheeded from the cab. "How you went to Hamilton's place, how you think you spotted Fredericks, how you both damn nearly got killed afterwards." His lips formed a tight line. "You've no real proof it was Hamilton."

"Is that the headquarters line?" queried Laird sarcastically.

Lundgard grunted. "They're not convinced. They're keener on the terrorist story—it makes more sense."

Laird shrugged. "How about you?"

"I don't know." Lundgard shook his head gloomily. "Maybe I'm more on your side." He scowled. "Did anything else happen last night? Nina—"

"What about her?" queried Laird.

"It was just a feeling I had. The way she was acting—as if she was holding something back." Lundgard looked at Laird for a moment, then flushed a little. "All right, forget it. That's not why I'm here. Andrew, talking about Hamilton is one thing. But I'm more worried about Professor Vassen. If he was involved—"

"If?" Laird grinned. "Now that's a long step forward."

"If," repeated Lundgard stubbornly. "You still think so?"

Laird nodded.

Lundgard swore sadly and took another swallow from the beer can. "I've got the afternoon off and there's another Berserkers rowing practice scheduled—from Tostig, where you saw us last time, right up the coast to Helsingor—we'll finish at the ferry terminal for Sweden."

"Is Vassen going along?"

"He'll be there to see us off. Then he's going by road and will meet us when we get there." Lundgard hesitated. "There have been a few cancellations among the crew for business reasons. The way things are, maybe I should call off too."

"It might be better if you went," mused Laird. He tried the coffee, but it was completely cold and he lit another cigarette instead. "It's your decision, Niels. But it would look more natural if you were aboard as usual—and it could be useful."

Lundgard thought, sighed, and nodded. "Karen is driving up to meet us at Helsingor—Chief Officer Peters is going with her. What about you?"

"I'm not exactly popular in Berserkers circles," reminded Laird. "But I might turn up."

"*Godt.*" Lundgard glanced at his wristwatch, took another long swallow from the beer can, then set it down. "I'll need to go. There was a warehouse robbery in the docks last night—some idiot drove off with a truckload of canned meat."

"Maybe he owns a big dog," suggested Laird.

Lundgard grunted. "I'm still the one who has to go along and make barking noises." He started towards the door, opened it, then stopped. "Our people drew a blank as far as Per Jensen is concerned—even at that jewellery store where he bought those earrings. They remember him being in, but they'd never seen him before."

"He still knew something," said Laird softly.

"And he got killed," reminded Lundgard grimly. "*Farvel.*"

He left, the door banging shut behind him. Laird took another draw on his cigarette, then stubbed it out, deciding he was smoking too much again.

Lundgard's longship trip only vaguely interested him. But for the moment he had time to kill before he could call Osgood Morris again. Suddenly, glad that Lundgard had gone, he made up his mind. The jewellery store near the Live Show club remained the only positive link with Jensen's death. At the very least, it would do no harm to look it over.

Fifteen minutes later he squeezed the rented Simca into a sidestreet parking place, got out, and walked the short distance to the jewellery store. It was a small, single-window shop not much more than a stone's-throw from the entrance to the Live Show.

The main door of the club was closed and the place looked deserted. But the same thing applied to much of the street. Late afternoon would probably be the time when that side of its business activity began to stir to life.

Hands in his pockets, Laird looked at the jewellery store's window display. Most of it was tourist-style cheap and nasty, with the price tags high. A tray of earrings like the pair Jensen had bought for his wife caught his eye and a slight grin crossed his lips as he saw their cost. Jensen, in character, had obviously beaten down the salesman to a discount price.

He turned, intending to enter the shop, then stopped and frowned. The entrance was split and formed two doors. One led into the jewellery store, the other served an office above. The name on the office doorway read AUSMAR VARIETY AGENCY, but what mattered more was the display board beside it.

The Ausmar Agency showed photographs of some of the alleged talent it handled, from singers and dancers to a small, grinning man who was dwarfed by a large performing dog. Right in the middle was a photograph of a buxom, dark-haired girl. It was "Lola from Madrid," the girl who had been in Hamilton's floor show the night before, and the caption under her photograph read "now booked, with other Ausmar stars, for a tour of U.S. clubs."

Laird stared at the photograph. A couple of girls, walking past, looked at the way he was studying it, nudged each other, and went on their way, giggling. But he hardly noticed them. His mind was racing, he had the feeling that he had just been handed an unexpected bonus—and he abandoned all notion of going into the jewellery store.

Instead, he went back to the Simca, got aboard, and

set it moving. He turned left at the end of the sidestreet, joined the main traffic flow, and tried to be patient at its crawling pace. He needed help on this one, and Sergeant Nina Kristensen was the best way of getting it.

The harbour police station was quiet when he got there. Laird left the Simca in the parking lot, went in, and drew a cheerful grin from the officer on desk duty as he headed for the detective section.

It was coffee time there, and several of the desks were occupied by plainclothesmen making feet-up telephone calls. Sergeant Kristensen was sitting with her back to the door, reading her way through a pile of report sheets, and he went up quietly and touched her on the shoulder.

"*God morgen,* Sergeant," he said with dry formality.

Sergeant Kristensen turned, surprised, then gave him an equally formal smile. She was back in her denim trousers and jacket and wearing dark glasses. The next desk was empty and Laird took its chair, brought it over, and sat opposite her.

"Why the glasses?" he asked.

Grimacing, she raised them briefly. One eye was swollen and half shut, but the other twinkled at him before the dark lenses came down again.

"A souvenir from last night," she said sadly.

"From *early* last night sounds better," he suggested.

She laughed. "*Ja.* Did you come to see Niels? He's out along the docks—I can get a message to him, but he probably won't be back here till tomorrow."

"I've seen him. That's not why I came."

Sergeant Kristensen frowned. "Have you heard from London?"

"Not yet." Laird paused as a couple of the plainclothesmen headed past them and went out. "Nina, I need some help. There's an Ausmar Variety Agency across the road from Hamilton's place. I want to know who owns it and how they operate—including how often they send artistes abroad."

"Now?"

He nodded.

It took two telephone calls, the first to a headquarters section and the second to a vice-squad contact. Both calls needed explanations, then Sergeant Kristensen had to wait till the voice at the other end came back with the answers. By the time she had finished, she had a page of scribbled notes in front of her and she set down the receiver with brisk satisfaction, though still slightly puzzled.

"You're going to find this interesting," she said dryly, studying her notes for a moment. "The Ausmar Agency is run by a Hans Frederick Ausmar—who also works nights as a compere at the Live Show club."

"Hans Frederick—who is probably our Fredericks." Laird whistled softly. "That's a bonus."

"*Ja*, but there's more, Andrew. Frederick Ausmar runs the agency but it is believed Hamilton probably owns it. Believed—there's no real proof."

"With Hamilton, there never is," said Laird grimly. "Does the Ausmar Agency send many people abroad?"

"A steady trickle, mostly small dance troupes—they've made it a specialty." She paused, a faint smile on her lips. "They're sending half a dozen girls on a short American tour in about three weeks time. Is that what you wanted?"

Laird slapped the desk hard, grinned, and nodded. Some of the other detectives in the room looked around at them, curious, then exchanged shrugs and went back to their own tasks.

"Can I phone London?" he asked.

"*Jeg be'r* . . . help yourself." She pushed the telephone across. "Just don't tell too many taxpayers."

He got through quickly to the Clanmore Alliance office in London, but then there was a delay. Osgood Morris was with the chairman, which in itself was encouraging. The marine-claims manager always headed for the board room when things were happening.

Laird waited, smoking a cigarette. Beside him, Sergeant Kristensen doodled patiently on her desk pad. She had sketched out the seventh in a fleet of miniature Viking longships when Morris' voice came on the line.

"Andrew?" He sounded particularly pleased with life. "This time you really have come up with something. The chairman has congratulated me, the entire insurance network is wanting to know more—"

"I'm glad for you," said Laird wearily. "But I'd like to know too. What have you got?"

"Your—ah—suggestion was right! We've gone back three years so far, and every time that Vassen exhibition was on a foreign visit the place they were at had a major robbery. A bank raid in Hamburg, the Lisbon casino safe blowing, that art theft in Florence—it goes on like that. Spring and autumn, just like we thought."

Laird grinned at the sudden "we" and asked, "Always while the Berserkers longship team was there?"

"Always," confirmed Morris happily. "Every case still unsolved, none of the stolen property recovered. Remember, it's incomplete. But insured losses we know about already top the half-million-pound mark. It's—damn them, it's the Viking raiders all over again."

"Viking thrust, they call it," said Laird stonily, but with a feeling of relief. At last he had a final shape. It was as cleverly conceived as anything he'd ever come across—and the motive behind it all was simple and single-minded.

"Andrew—" A faint note of concern entered Morris'

voice. "My Scotland Yard contact is screaming about tell-ing Interpol."

"Stall him," said Laird. He winked at Sergeant Kris-tensen. "Tell him if he waits he'll have it as one neat pack-age, courtesy of the Danish police."

"With Clanmore getting a share of the credit," re-minded Morris quickly. "All right, I'll talk to him. Ah—what's the chance of loss recovery? Clanmore isn't heavily involved because that kind of risk cover isn't our scene. But the other companies want to know."

"Tell them not to count on it being easy," said Laird bluntly. "I think I know where the money ended up—but it could be one hell of a job ever proving it."

Laird said goodbye, hung up, and felt tired. Despite what he'd told Morris, the hardest part could still lie ahead. Then he realised Sergeant Kristensen was watching him, waiting.

"London say yes—it matches." He told Morris' end of the conversation while she sat silent, her chin on her hands, listening carefully. "Like to hear my guess at how it adds up?"

She nodded soberly. "A lot of people are going to want to know. In Copenhagen, when you talk about Harald Vassen you talk about an institution."

"That's going to be somebody else's worry," he said grimly. "Every time the Berserkers oarsmen have gone abroad spring and autumn there's been a major robbery in that city. The kind that was planned before they went—probably by Vassen himself or by whoever was sent out to make the official exhibition recce visit."

"We can check that out, get names," she agreed.

"Later," he said, nodding. "Then the few people in-volved pull the job during the rowing-team visit—and the rest of the team don't know a thing about it. Back here, they've got Hamilton waiting to fence the stuff for them. But they don't want to run the risk of being caught bringing it into Denmark when they return. That's where the Ausmar Agency probably comes in—and that's what Per Jensen probably stumbled on before they killed him."

"Showgirls." Sergeant Kristensen's lips shaped a silent appreciation. "A bunch of showgirls coming back from abroad."

"Even customs officers are human," mused Laird. "They'd be too busy looking at the girls' legs to worry about their luggage—maybe the girls didn't even know they were bringing in anything extra."

"And the same thing was planned for Boston." She frowned at him through her dark glasses.

"Boston and maybe New York. My guess would be both." Laird rubbed a hand along his chin, the next part an amalgam of circumstance and possibility. "But things started to go wrong during the run-up time. I'm still betting Hamilton wanted a bigger cut, that Vassen said no, and that the *Velella* fire was a threat and a warning from Hamilton. Right now they're probably one stage short of open war."

"With casualties." Sergeant Kristensen looked away from him, tapped a finger on her desk for a moment, then faced him again. "When I spoke to headquarters they told me they'd been keeping a loose surveillance watch on Peter Hamilton. But they've lost him—all they know is he drove out of the city this morning with three men, heading north. He hasn't been seen since."

"Heading north—" Laird swore under his breath. "Did Niels tell you Vassen's plans?"

She shook her head.

"Vassen will see the longship off from Tostig this afternoon. Then he's driving north to Helsingor, to meet them later."

He didn't need to spell the rest out. It could mean a meeting had been arranged between the two men, an attempt at a settlement so that they could get back to business.

"What about it, Nina?" he asked quietly. "Niels will be at the longship and though he'll hate it like hell, that's where he should stay. But if you and I followed Vassen—"

She frowned at the telephone. "*Ja*, except that I should tell headquarters—tell them now."

"Official channels?" He raised a sardonic eyebrow. "How easily are they going to accept that your much-loved Professor Vassen is almost certainly on the crook?" Then he had an idea. "Tell them you've got a possible line on Hamilton and you'd like to check it out. That should be easier—and it could give you some help in the background."

Sergeant Nina Kristensen nodded and reached for the telephone.

CHAPTER SEVEN

The sky stayed grey, the wind stayed fresh, and there was an occasional drizzle of rain as Andrew Laird drove the rented Simca north. At one o'clock he reached the shore road which led down to Tostig village, slowed to a crawl, and glanced in his rear mirror. Sergeant Kristensen's little M.G. was not far behind and it slowed in turn. Then a single flash came from the M.G.'s headlamps before it pulled off the road and stopped out of sight behind a screen of bushes.

Satisfied, Laird set the Simca moving again. Minutes later he reached the village pier and stopped the car in one of the few spaces left in the parking area. The Viking longship was bobbing beside the pier in the low, white-flecked swell coming in from the Øresund Strait and despite the grey sky there was an almost picnic aspect about the scene. The coastal trip ahead had brought out a small audience of relatives and friends to watch the oarsmen leave.

He slung what looked like a small camera case over his shoulder, left the car, and walked towards the pier. On the way, he passed the tan-coloured Volvo station wagon. It was empty, but it was a reminder that he had to go carefully —and a moment later, easing through the groups of people standing near the longship, he saw Harald Vassen ahead.

Vassen saw him, too. The man's wrinkled face froze; he gave Laird a look which held no welcome, then he moved away.

A voice hailed him. Laird glanced around, saw Niels Lundgard beckoning a little way ahead, and pushed his way through another group to reach the Dane. Lundgard already had company. Karen Leslie, in trousers and a heavy sweater, smiled a greeting. At her side stood Chief Officer Peters, looking slightly bemused by his surroundings. His burned hand was still bandaged, but he was holding a camera in the other.

"*Tak,* Andrew . . . thanks for coming," said Lundgard cheerfully. He thumbed at the other groups around. "I was beginning to feel lonely until Karen showed up—everyone else seems to have brought a fan club."

"I'll get your autograph later," said Laird. He glanced at Sean Peters. "You're the professional. Would you go out with them?"

"In that?" Peters blinked at the longship and shook his head. "No further than I could swim."

"Where's your spirit of adventure, Sean?" demanded Karen.

"All used up." Peters pointed to Laird's camera case. "Taking pictures?"

"No, I'm going to ask Niels to take some for me along the way," said Laird easily. "I've got to go in a moment."

Peters shrugged. "I'll get mine here, then more at Helsingor—we'll be there to see them come in." He turned to Karen. "Like to help, girl? There isn't much time."

Nodding, she went away with him. Once they had gone, Lundgard's smile died and he lowered his voice.

"*Hvad* . . . what's happening, Andrew?" he asked quietly. "When I got here, the village constable met me with a message from headquarters. I was to stay with the longship whatever happened, and you'd meet me. Nothing else, except that it involved Hamilton—"

"Hamilton and Harald Vassen," said Laird bluntly. "It looks like they're meeting—and there's a positive tie-up." He saw Lundgard's question coming and shook his head. "Sorry, Niels, it'll have to wait. But there could be trouble— anywhere."

"And I draw the longship." Lundgard twisted a brief, bitter grin. "Who do I thank for that?"

"You'll be where they'd expect you to be." Laird side-stepped the question. He let a party of oarsmen go by, then took the camera case from his shoulder and gave it to Lundgard. "You'll need this. Nina says the set inside will send and receive up to ten kilometres. No transmissions either way unless it's vital."

"Understood." Lundgard slung the case and the radio it concealed over his shoulder. "Anything else?"

"I saw Vassen along the pier. How about his large friend Bermann? Is he crewing today?"

"*Nej*. He's here, but only to see us off." He hesitated. "I know Professor Vassen has a cottage somewhere along the coast—but I don't know where."

"That could be it," mused Laird.

A whistle blew and Lundgard frowned. "We've to get aboard. That's the signal."

"And I'm leaving," Laird told him. "Happy rowing."

Lundgard swore at him sadly, then forced a smile and hefted the camera bag.

"*Tak*, Andrew," he said loudly. "I'll try to get you some good pictures."

Turning, he joined the other oarsmen who were start-ing to clamber aboard the longship to their places on the rowing benches. Taking his time, Laird began to walk back towards the parking lot. On the way, he reached a spot

where Sean Peters was taking photographs with Karen Leslie in their foreground.

"I've got to get back to town," he told them easily.
"Velella claim forms, Sean—the sooner they're processed
the sooner you can forget about them."

He left them, saw Harald Vassen again, but still hadn't
spotted Bermann or the blond oarsman's two usual companions when he reached the Simca. Starting the engine, he
took a last glance back towards the longship. It was easing
away from the pier, the long banks of oars lowering for
their first dip into the water.

His mouth tightened a little at the sight. A lot was lia-
ble to happen before that dragon prow reached Helsingor.

———————————

A few minutes later Andrew Laird bumped the Simca
off the road and went in behind the screen of bushes where
Sergeant Kristensen was waiting in her M.G. He left his car,
crossed over, and got in beside her. Resting on the gearbox
hump between them was a twin of the little radio he'd given
Lundgard.

"Any problems?" she asked, elbows leaning on the
steering wheel and a calmly practical note in her voice.

"None." He took out his cigarettes, lit two, and put
one between her lips. "I saw Niels and he knows what to
do. Vassen is down there too."

She nodded absently. "Did Niels say anything?"

"He didn't exactly send friendly greetings," Laird admitted.

Sergeant Kristensen gave a soft, sympathetic laugh,
then stopped and pointed. Where they were hidden, they
could still see a stretch of the road—the road any traffic
leaving Tostig would have to use. But beyond that they had

a view of a section of the inlet, and the longship had just come into sight. Her single sail had been hoisted and was straining in the wind, aiding the steady rhythm of the long oars propelling her out towards the Øresund Strait.

In less than a minute the Viking ship had vanished again. Soon afterwards, the first cars began driving past their hiding place as spectators began leaving Tostig. Laird smoked in silence, exchanging a glance with Sergeant Kristensen when one went past with Karen Leslie at the wheel and Sean Peters in the passenger seat.

But he stayed silent, with plenty to think about. The Danish police were being cautious, reluctant to show any kind of hand until more in the way of hard fact was available. He didn't blame them—but if that didn't happen or anything went wrong, then he had no illusions about his own position.

For the moment he was useful, and that was why they were letting him stay involved. If there was trouble, then he'd suddenly become a foreign civilian who had been acting without their knowledge.

Laird grinned a little. He'd have played it the same way. A few additional police patrol cars had been quietly injected into the area between Tostig and Helsingor, but there was no other backup.

Look but don't touch—it was being spelled out clearly.

Suddenly, Sergeant Kristensen gave a murmur and quickly stubbed out her cigarette on the dashboard ashtray. He did the same, seeing the tan Volvo station wagon sweeping up the road towards them.

As it passed, tyres crunching on the gravel, they could see the big blond figure of Bermann at the wheel. There was one man beside him and Harald Vassen sat alone and upright in the back.

The M.G.'s engine throbbed to life and Sergeant Kristensen smartly reversed the little car out of hiding. She flicked the gear lever into first but kept the clutch pedal down and glanced at Laird.

"Now, Nina," he said softly. "But give him room."

They bounced forward onto the road and started after the station wagon, which was already a toylike shape ahead. As it reached the junction with the main road, the right-hand turn indicator began blinking.

"Heading north," said Laird with relief.

"*Ja.*" Sergeant Kristensen spared a glance from the road and smiled at him. "What else?"

They followed the Volvo out on the northern route. Traffic was light, the tan-coloured station wagon ahead was in no hurry, and it was an easy task to keep it in sight. Laird relaxed back and let the kilometres go by. He'd left Tostig in the Simca and he knew he must have been watched. But if anyone in the car ahead did glance back, the little open car would most likely be ignored—or taken to be just one of the usual flow of vehicles heading for the Swedish ferry-crossing terminal at Helsingor.

Their route stayed close to the shore. Out on the grey water of the Øresund, the dragon ship was somewhere far behind them. But there was plenty of other traffic, from distant white specks which were ferries on the Swedish run to a large oil tanker inward bound for Copenhagen. Laird eyed the tanker with a mixture of envy and sympathy for her crew. Tanker life was a mixture of danger and boredom but just sometimes he wished he was back on a deck again—any deck. There, at least, the world was a compact, practical place with clear-cut rules.

"Andrew." Sergeant Kristensen said his name like a quiet warning and nodded ahead, already easing back on the accelerator.

The Volvo was slowing. Red brake lights winked, then

it swung down a narrow track which led towards the shore. The station wagon disappeared into a thick screen of trees and beyond the trees Laird caught a glimpse of a red-tiled roof.

"Keep going, Nina," he advised. "They could have a lookout posted back there."

She kept the M.G. moving but stopped about half a kilometre on, where she could pull off the road on a narrow strip of grass beside a small stream. Switching off the engine, she took the little radio transmitter and stuffed it into her leather shoulderbag.

"Ready?" she asked calmly.

They left the car. The stream flowed through a belt of thick scrub in the direction of the strip of woodland, and they began following it, tramping through the long, wet grass while flying insects of all kinds, from occasional buzzing wasps to a multitude of small black flies, pestered around them. There was a simple stob-and-wire fence at the start of the trees and they climbed over it, then paused. Swearing under her breath, Sergeant Kristensen brushed away more of the flies.

"*Hvor* . . . where now?" she asked.

"To the right somewhere." Laird tried to take a bearing from the road behind them. "We should be fairly near." A wasp buzzed him and he flicked it away. "I'll go on and take a look."

"*Nej.*" She shook her head firmly. "We'll both take a look. You try to the right, I'll keep straight on. Then we can meet back here."

He didn't argue, and looked around again. The woodland seemed empty except for the insects and a few birds. The loudest sound was the murmur of the stream as it flowed on towards the sea.

"Fifteen minutes, then," he agreed. "And we stay clear of trouble."

She was gone before he could say anything more. Shrugging, he flicked at the wasp as it came back again, then started off on his own route.

The trees were a mixture of spruce and pine and the ground around their roots was a litter of twigs and cones. Laird moved carefully, knowing how the sound of a snapped twig could travel and uncertain of what it might disturb. A rabbit scampered across his path, and once, to his left, he caught a brief flicker of blue denim as Sergeant Kristensen crossed a gap.

But that was all, and suddenly he was at the edge of the wood and close to the red-roofed house. It was small, with white walls and a blue door, and beyond it the ground fell away rapidly towards a narrow sea cove where a small power boat lay moored beside a plank jetty.

Laird grinned. Two cars were parked in the driveway close to the house door, the tan Volvo and Peter Hamilton's grey Mercedes-Benz—and there was no sign of their occupants.

Sitting back on his heels for a moment, he decided he could get closer. He half rose, ready to crawl forward through the bushes, then froze where he was as a swift rustle of movement came from behind him. Before he could even turn, the unmistakable muzzle of a gun jabbed firmly against his backbone.

"*Lan somt* . . . slowly," murmured an amused, derisive voice. "On your feet. Don't look around—hands on your head."

Helpless, he obeyed, and was rewarded with a grunt.

"Start walking." The gun jabbed an emphasis. "Straight for the house. Stop on the driveway."

Again he had to obey, cursing his carelessness. As they

reached the driveway and stopped, he risked a glance over his shoulder. The gun muzzle jabbed deeper in a final warning but before he faced front again he had time to see that it was one of Hamilton's slim young bouncers from the Live Show club.

The man behind him shouted. A moment passed, then the door of the house flew open and Hamilton's pimple-faced driver came out with a gun in his hand. The gun at Laird's back jabbed him on again and the two men escorted him through the door, then into a large, plainly furnished room which had a big stone open fireplace as its main feature.

There was no trace of a welcome from the four men already in the room. Standing beside the fireplace, Peter Hamilton considered him with a scowl. The black-haired, gold-toothed man who called himself Fredericks was nearby, beside the big, blond figure of Bermann, both showing no reaction, waiting for a lead. But the real surprise was Harald Vassen, who was slumped in a chair with blood trickling from a cut lip. He hardly glanced at Laird, then his eyes switched back to Hamilton in a way that held a strange, burning fury.

"Where did you find him?" asked Hamilton curtly.

"Over in the trees." The Live Show bouncer gave a self-congratulatory grin. "He didn't know a thing till it happened."

"Check him, Carl," Hamilton told his driver. That took a moment, with Laird unceremoniously jammed against a wall while he was frisked. The man silently indicated that he was finished and Hamilton glanced at the bouncer again. "You're sure he was alone?"

"*Ja.* I saw him come through the trees."

Hamilton grunted. "What about it, Laird?"

"I was passing by and I thought I'd drop in," said

Laird mildly, then winced as the driver slapped him back-handed across the mouth.

"Outside, both of you," ordered Hamilton. "Stay near the house and keep your eyes open. We'll collect his car later."

Nodding, they went out. Hamilton had his hands in his pockets and was scowling, but Laird's attention had switched to Harald Vassen, who still hadn't moved from his chair, and then on to Bermann. The blond oarsman had drawn a gun, the muzzle pointing negligently in his direction.

"I see I came at the wrong time," said Laird sadly, and glanced around. "Someone's missing. Vassen, where's your other little friend?"

"Ask them," said Vassen in a bitter voice. His wrinkled, blood-smeared face twisted angrily. "They dragged him out of here—for all I know, he's dead."

"*Nej,* he's not dead, you old fool," said the gold-toothed man sardonically. "Not yet—so stop whining."

Harald Vassen gripped the arms of his chair. For a moment Laird thought the small, grey-haired figure was going to erupt across the room; then, sighing, Vassen slumped back again. Turning, Laird saw the expressions on the other faces around him and understood.

"Under new management?" he asked Hamilton flatly, and didn't wait for an answer. "Well, I've met Bermann before—Bermann, The Ape to his friends, right? But what about your tame entertainer with the agency sideline? Do I call him Fredericks or Ausmar?"

"Fredericks will do." Hamilton's soft voice held a new note of interest but his heavy face had tightened. "Maybe you're more of a problem than I thought."

"Not enough, or I wouldn't be here," said Laird wryly.

A nervous laugh came from Bermann. Bull neck reddening at the sound, Hamilton swung around on the blond oarsman and silenced him with a glare. Then, suddenly, he took two steps forward and shoved Laird backwards into a chair beside Vassen.

"All right, Laird," he said curtly. "Why did you come here? And I want a straight answer. I've no time for games."

"It looks that way," agreed Laird and shrugged. "I just didn't go along with the story about naughty terrorists wanting to set off bombs. The way I see it, the Vikings have been raiding again—with you handling the business end."

Hamilton considered him silently for a moment, then gave a grim nod, went back to Fredericks, and began talking in a low voice. Taking a deep breath, Laird looked around the room again.

It had one big window, which faced the front of the house and the trees beyond. There was a desk at the window and near it a painting of Vassen as a young man hung above a glass-fronted display cabinet filled with Viking relics. A Viking axe, very similar to the one in Vassen's townhouse, was on display above the stone fireplace.

For the moment, none of it mattered much. He glanced at the window again. Harald Vassen's coastal retreat had become a death trap and his one hope lay out among those trees, with Sergeant Kristensen. The odds were that she had seen him marched into the house at gunpoint. She had the radio and at least one of the extra patrol cars must be near the area. But there were still two armed men out there on the edge of the wood.

It was a gamble, with the odds hard to assess.

"Professor," he said deliberately, and waited till Vassen looked up. "You had a good thing going. But I'll bet even the old-time Vikings had an occasional rotten apple in the barrel."

"When it happened, they knew how to deal with them," said Vassen hoarsely. He moistened his cut lip while his eyes switched to Bermann and his face showed total contempt. "I was a fool. I trusted the wrong man."

Bermann gave an uneasy grin, tightening his grip on the gun in his hand, and glanced at Hamilton.

"You know your real problem, Vassen?" asked Hamilton, amused. He thumbed towards the old battle-axe above the fireplace. "You think everybody should worship junk like that thing the way you do. With me, if a man takes risks then I pay out—he gets more than the small change for expenses."

"You pay," agreed Laird neutrally. "Bermann, did he tell you the kind of bonus your pal Pittner drew for the firebomb on the *Velella*? A rigged timer—he got his share all right. The hard way."

"Pittner was a risk," said Bermann unhappily. "He drank too much—and sometimes he talked."

"Forget the history lesson," grunted Hamilton impatiently. "Bermann, we've a job down at the beach. Fredericks will cope with these two."

Fredericks showed his gold tooth in a humourless grin of agreement. He was holding a gun, a heavy Colt .38 Magnum revolver, and he dragged an upright chair over to face Laird and Vassen, then sat down. There was a silencer screwed on the end of the barrel. Then he fished a thin, crumpled cigarette from his top pocket, lit it, and the sickly sweet scent of marijuana drifted in the air.

"Leaving us with the professional?" Laird asked Hamilton bleakly.

"Ask him," said Hamilton, grinning. Then, beckoning Bermann, he led the way out of the room. A moment later they heard the outside door open and close, then the two men went past the window, heading around the side of the house.

Vassen shifted in his chair. Immediately, the revolver in Fredericks' hand twitched a fraction, the muzzle training on Vassen's scrawny middle.

"*Nej* . . . just behave," he said lazily. "This gun makes just a little hole when it goes in—but a very large one when it comes out the other side."

"Like it did with Jensen?" asked Laird softly.

"He was careless about where he asked questions." Fredericks shrugged. "But he died quickly. A bullet in the stomach would be slower—remember that."

"Thanks." Laird knew the warning was real. "Suppose I reach for my cigarettes?"

"You reach for nothing." Fredericks gave a bored half yawn.

"Can we talk?" Laird nodded towards Vassen.

"*Ja.* If you don't move." Fredericks sat back, the revolver held unwaveringly.

"What was supposed to happen here, Professor?" asked Laird after a moment. "A new deal with Hamilton?"

"So I thought," said Vassen wearily. "Bermann and Olaf came with me—"

"What happened to their other pal?" queried Laird.

A sad smile touched Vassen's lined face. "He has been sick since he fought with you outside my house. He stayed at home—he was lucky. When we got here, Hamilton told me what was going to happen. Harald Vassen is going to disappear, Bermann will take over the longship team—"

"Just like that?" Laird raised an eyebrow.

"It can be managed," said Vassen slowly. "The Berserkers members would probably accept it. They have seen Bermann in charge before, when I couldn't be with them."

He sighed. "I tried to hit Hamilton. Then Olaf tried to help me and—"

"And he got a pistol barrel over his head," said Fredericks, grinning, from his chair. "Tell him who did it, Vassen."

"Bermann." Harald Vassen nodded bitterly, his hands tightening again at the memory. "Laird, you say you know what we have been doing. But do you know why?"

"Those 'anonymous' donations to the trust." Laird saw the grin spreading over Fredericks' face again. "How much went there?"

"Everything—after a third share to Hamilton for handling and disposal and our own expenses." Vassen's anger began gathering again at the same time as something like an appeal entered his voice. "I was turning a dream into reality."

"You mean everything was fine till your luck ran out," said Laird stonily.

"We had to get money," persisted Vassen. "Do you think I could have built up the trust and the Vassen Collection to what it is now on ordinary donations?"

"You might have tried," said Laird dryly.

"I did at first." Vassen's face tightened. "Then I decided the Vikings would have to raid again. I picked four men, all former students of mine—men I believed had the kind of outlook I needed."

"Then you fed them into the rowing team, with a raid lined up every time the Berserkers went on tour." Laird felt he wanted a cigarette more than ever. "What was scheduled at Boston?"

"A bank raid—an easy one." Vassen grimaced. "I made the preparations when I was over there last month."

"But you didn't reckon on Hamilton," mused Laird. "When did he get involved?"

"We used him almost from the beginning, because we needed a way to dispose of the things we brought back—"

"You mean you needed a fence," said Laird brutally.

Vassen nodded uncomfortably. "Aksel Pittner knew about him and made contact. At first, Hamilton didn't even know who he was working for—but he found out. Then we used him more, and eventually he wasn't satisfied."

Fredericks chuckled at the words and they looked around.

"What the old man means is Hamilton is taking over," said Fredericks lazily. His gun moved in a casual emphasis. "It'll be the same operation, but no more charity stuff."

"I came here today prepared to offer him a full half share," said Vassen bitterly. "That was what he wanted before—and when I refused, he warned me I'd regret it."

"The fire on the *Velella*?"

"*Ja*. Afterwards, he told me the Vassen Collection could be destroyed just as easily as the dragon ship had been burned. Then I knew I had to make peace with him, I couldn't take that risk." Vassen bit his lip. "I'd already had one shock—discovering that Aksel Pittner had been working for him. But right up till we got here today I never dreamed that Bermann would—" He stopped and sighed.

Laird nodded, then glanced over at Fredericks.

"What happens next?" he asked.

Fredericks gave a fractional shrug and didn't answer.

Another couple of minutes passed, then Hamilton and Bermann returned to the house. Both looked windblown and Hamilton was breathing heavily. When he came into the room he looked around and frowned.

"Has Carl come back?" he demanded.

"Nej . . . but you told them to stay out." Lazily, Fredericks tossed his thin cigarette into the fireplace and rose to his feet. "Want me to go and look for them?"

"Later." Hamilton turned to Bermann and thumbed towards the door. "Get the other one."

Bermann went away and came back half dragging, half pushing a swaying figure. It was the other oarsman who had come with Vassen. His hands were tied behind his back, his head was caked with dried blood, and he could barely stand when Bermann released his grip. Grinning, Fredericks pushed him and he fell to the floor with a moan.

"You're going on a boat trip, all three of you," said Hamilton shortly, his broad face impassive. "Vassen's boat —the story will be that you left here with the notion you'd go out and meet the longship as it went rowing past." His mouth twisted a little. "Except that you must have met a patch of rough sea. Because you didn't get there."

"And we just disappear?" Laird felt his mouth go dry but forced a cynical note into his voice. "Too crude—it wouldn't work."

"It will. Because Bermann here will take the Volvo into Helsingor and make worried noises straight away—that he warned you against the idea but Vassen wouldn't listen." Hamilton gave a short laugh. "And everybody knows Harald Vassen when he's in a stubborn mood."

Vassen's face had gone almost as grey as his hair. But his head came up fiercely.

"And the police?" he demanded. "Won't they start asking questions again, like they did before?"

"Tell him, Bermann," invited Hamilton sardonically.

"Ja." Bermann looked pleased with himself. "It was my idea—another firebomb tonight, in the docks. It will keep them too busy chasing terrorists to have other thoughts."

Laird looked at Harald Vassen and saw only a tired resignation. Then Bermann was shoving them towards the man lying on the floor.

"Pick him up," ordered Hamilton curtly.

They did, with Bermann and Fredericks in close attendance, their guns ready. Silently, Hamilton thumbed them towards the door, then froze where he was, giving a startled grunt. Outside the window, his pimple-faced driver had appeared from the trees and was coming towards the house in a desperate, stumbling run.

Fredericks swore and Bermann stood with his mouth hanging open as two other figures broke from the wood in pursuit. At the same moment as Laird recognised them as a police patrolman and Sergeant Kristensen, the pimple-faced driver spun around and brought up the gun in his hand.

Two shots rang out. Dropping down on one knee, Nina Kristensen held her pistol in a steady, two-handed marksman grip and fired once in return.

The pimple-faced driver fell, then writhed on the ground, clutching his leg.

Two more patrolmen crashed out of the wood and the paralysis which had gripped the spectators in the house ended. Cursing, Fredericks swung his Magnum .38, aiming at Sergeant Kristensen's blue-denim-clad figure—and simultaneously Laird hurled himself sideways and slammed against the man.

They went sprawling together while the soft plop of the silenced revolver brought a smash of glass and the window disintegrated. Rolling as he fell, Fredericks fired again but this time the heavy bullet simply gouged plaster as it buried itself in the wall.

Somewhere in the background Laird heard a car skidding to a halt outside in a squeal of brakes. But it hardly registered—because the small, grey figure of Harald Vassen had exploded across the room. Vassen had let go the semi-conscious oarsman he'd been supporting and as the man slumped he'd rushed past the still-stupefied Bermann.

Three steps took Harald Vassen to the stone fireplace. His hands ripped the ancient Viking battle-axe from its place, then he turned with an unearthly, bubbling cry of rage. Held two-handed, the axe rose in a swinging arc.

Fredericks was scrambling up as Bermann, wide-eyed with terror, triggered his pistol. Two short, sharp reports rang out at pointblank range but Harald Vassen barely staggered—then the steel axe blade descended on Bermann, taking the big blond oarsman between neck and shoulder, sheering through flesh and bone in a terrible, blood-spouting blow.

Wrenching the axe free as Bermann fell, Harald Vassen sought a new target while the strange, bubbling cry came again from deep in his scrawny throat. He made for Fredericks, the axe rising for another terrible, two-handed blow.

Backing away, Fredericks shot him three times at close range. Each time Vassen's thin frame jerked as if hit by a giant hammer. His legs buckled—but the axe still completed its final, glinting arc.

Fredericks didn't have time to scream. The blade split its way through his skull as if meeting kindling wood.

Then, suddenly, it was over. The only sound in the room was a low moaning from the young oarsman. He was moving feebly, trying to sit upright.

Bermann was dead, Fredericks was dead. Harald Vassen lay where he had fallen, one hand still touching the handle of the axe. And the rest was blood-spattered carnage.

Rising, Laird looked around and felt ready to vomit. But he couldn't see Hamilton—and as the fact was still registering he heard feet pounding through the hallway. A moment later, a squad of police poured in with guns drawn. Sergeant Kristensen was with them, her face gaunt with anxiety.

"Andrew—" She saw him and relief shone in her bright blue eyes. "You're all right?"

He nodded. One of the patrolmen went past them a couple of steps, looked down at Fredericks, and turned away green-faced.

"Did you get Hamilton?" asked Laird urgently.

"*Nej.*" She spoke quickly to the patrolmen and they scattered to search the house. "No one came out. We heard the shots and I thought—"

"Thank Vassen." Laird drew a deep, still-unbelieving breath. "He went *berserker,* Nina." He managed a lopsided grin. "You saw them bring me in?"

"*Ja.* So I radioed for help and got back to the road. Two patrol cars weren't far away," she said thankfully. "We were coming through the wood, almost at the house, when we bumped into Hamilton's men. One gave up, the other—" She shook her head.

"Does Niels Lundgard know?"

She nodded. "He's on his way."

A shout came from the back of the house and a patrolman carrying a carbine hurried into the room. He spoke briefly, and she swung around again.

"There's a rear door lying open, Andrew—and a path to the beach."

Laird understood and cursed himself. "There's a boat down there, a fast one—"

They ran from the house, two of the patrolmen at their heels. Pounding down the steeply sloping path, Laird saw the grey water of the inlet ahead, then Hamilton standing on the plankboard jetty. The man was struggling to free the mooring lines, managed it a moment later, and jumped aboard.

Sprinting on, Laird heard the engine growl to life. The small craft began to foam away from the jetty, turning fast in the narrow inlet, swinging out to face a light sea mist drifting in with the wind from the Øresund Strait.

The patrolman with the carbine fired a shot. Crouching low over the powerboat's control, Hamilton didn't look back. The patrolman aimed again, but Sergeant Kristensen knocked the carbine aside.

At the same instant, the boat's engine faltered and slowed.

The mouth of the inlet was no longer empty. Silently, like some vengeful wraith, a tall dragon prow was bearing down out of the light sea mist. The Viking longship came rippling on, her long banks of oars raised from the water.

A slow drumbeat began. The oars came to life, dipped and rose, dipped and rose again while that dragon prow came around to bear on the powerboat. There was no way past her.

The powerboat had stopped in the water. They could see Hamilton staring ahead while the drumbeat continued its slow throb and the longship came relentlessly on.

Suddenly, the boat engine came to life again. Hamilton swung the tiller and steered dejectedly back towards the jetty. When he got there, he climbed out, raised his hands above his head, and waited.

Laird reached him at the same time as the patrolman.

"I don't carry a gun," said Hamilton wearily as he was frisked. Then he turned his head, staring at the longship, his mouth twisted in a tight, bitter disbelief. "They'd have killed me out there. You know that."

He was being handcuffed when Niels Lundgard

splashed ashore from the longship, which had grounded in the shallows.

Lundgard hit him once, backhanded, across the face. Then they left him there with the patrolmen and went back up to the house.

———————

Harald Vassen should have been dead. He had five bullet wounds in his frail body, his lifeblood was ebbing, but somehow he still clung to a spark of life. A cushion had been placed under his head by one of the patrolmen and he managed a weak imitation of a smile as Laird and Lundgard bent over him.

"Hamilton?" he asked in a whisper.

"We have him," said Lundgard reassuringly. "Lie still, an ambulance is coming."

"I won't need it. But make—make sure they look after Olaf." Vassen stifled a cough and looked across at the young oarsman who had been beaten up by Hamilton's men. He was being helped onto a couch by another of the patrolmen. "*Ja*, he stayed loyal to me."

"He has a brother," said Lundgard quietly. "They do most things together."

"So you know my fourth man." Vassen grimaced painfully. "But whatever they did, I—I take all blame." He fought for breath for a moment. "Remember that, Niels—I want it known."

Lundgard nodded.

"Laird—" Vassen twitched a finger, beckoning him closer. "Remember I told you—told you about the old Viking ways?" His words were beginning to slur and he coughed again, a choking sound. "Retribution—Fredericks and Bermann. Remember what I said."

"To kiss the thin lips of the axe," said Laird quietly. "I remember."

"*Ja.*" Vassen almost smiled. "*På gensyn*, Niels—"

The words ended in a short, bubbling sigh and his head fell limp.

"*På gensyn* . . . till the next time," said Niels Lundgard softly. Then he rose and walked away.

Five days later Andrew Laird stood in the departure lounge at Copenhagen's International Airport. The S.A.S. afternoon flight to Boston and New York had just been called and Karen Leslie was saying goodbye.

He smiled as he watched Chief Officer Peters gravely kiss her on the cheek. The *Velella* had unloaded and was now in drydock for repair. When the ship was ready for service again, Peters would wear his captain's braid.

It had been a turmoil of a five days. Hours spent giving statements to a procession of Danish officials, more hours dictating reports for Clanmore Alliance—with in the middle of it all Osgood Morris flying in for a brief, edgy visit. The marine-claims-department manager never liked being out of London but the chairman had sent him, so Morris had tried to be pleasant.

What would happen to the Vassen Trust was another matter. Accountants and lawyers were already gathering around that problem; how much of it would survive wouldn't be decided for a long time ahead. Shock and disbelief and newspaper headlines had given way to unruffled Scandinavian thoroughness.

The state prosecutor's department was busy too. The charges against Peter Hamilton were still growing. The Live Show club was closed, and several of his men shared cells in the same prison block where he would stay till he was tried.

The two surviving members of Harald Vassen's team of Viking raiders were there too, but talking freely, almost proudly, while robbery files in half a dozen countries were reopened and Interpol's telecommunications department sweated out the results.

Laird glanced at Niels Lundgard. The long-faced Dane wore his best suit and was holding Karen Leslie's hand. Lundgard's trip with the Berserkers rowing team to America was off—but only temporarily. The oarsmen had met, had begun by talking about disbanding, and had finished by deciding they'd stay together, fix new dates, and face the world.

He grinned. By his own reckoning, they would now be the biggest draw any promoter was ever likely to lay hands on.

The S.A.S. flight announcement came again, a shade more impatiently. Karen Leslie came towards him, with Lundgard still at her side.

"Goodbye, Andrew." She smiled at him, her copper hair glinting under the airport lights. "You still disappoint me."

"Why?" He could guess the answer.

"That other girl." She frowned. "I wanted to know."

"Long ago and far away," he said easily. "You've got the edge on her anyway."

She kissed him hard on the lips, then winked at Lundgard. The Dane grinned, took her hand again, and they went over to the departure gate.

Lighting a cigarette, Laird went out and took his place on the long rolling pavement with a mixture of newly arrived passengers. The sun poured in through the windows along the way and as he neared the main terminal lobby he saw Sergeant Kristensen waiting. She wore a light cotton dress which clung to her figure and her blond hair was tied back by a crisp white ribbon.

"Did you fix it?" he asked, putting an arm around her waist.

"Ja." She nodded demurely. "A week's leave. I said I had an aunt who was ill. But just one thing—"

"I know," he agreed. "I don't call you Sergeant."

Her old M.G. was at the kerb outside the terminal's doors, lying neatly between two *Parkering Forbudt* signs. Laird grinned as he saw that his suitcase was already in the back.

The airport paging system came to life. Andrew Laird was wanted at the main inquiry desk, to take a telephone call from London.

"Another time, Osgood," said Laird mildly.

Then he helped Nina Kristensen into the car.